Gramma.... is

Jonas Lane

Grammarticus

Jonas Lane

Published by Jonas Lane Writing Ltd. 2019

Contents

Grammarticus

About the author

Jonas Lane loves to combine his love of writing and teaching.

This novel grew from the conversations he had with the young writers who Jonas works with. The main aim of his workshops is to inspire frustrated young writers to write creatively, as well as instilling in them a love of writing which is often driven out of them by the over-zealous demands of a grammar-based curriculum.

Grammarticus grew from his own frustrations felt when he himself was at school and, much later, whilst teaching.

He hopes that it will serve as a reminder to everyone that your best is nearly always good enough.

Jonas lives with his wife, mad dog and crazy cats in a secret location, far away from the grammar police…

Visit Jonas at his website

www.jonaslaneauthor.com

For all my young writers...

This was only supposed to be a short story but became something magical, causing me much mischief and mayhem!

J.L. x

Chapter 1

Everywhere that Zach Turner looked there were words.

Words scrawled on the whiteboard.

Words that seemed to decorate every single blank space in the classroom.

Words that filled the PowerPoint presentation which seemed to be travelling at a thousand miles an hour as Miss Fletcher continued to drone on, her high pitched, nasally voice whining, an incessant buzzing in Zach's ears that refused to go away.

He was bored and confused.

Bored at the monotonous lessons he was being forced to endure day in, day out.

Confused by the amount of information that he was expected to take in just to supposedly be able to write his sentences correctly.

Zach knew that he wasn't alone in his feelings. There were plenty of his friends in Year 6 who felt exactly the same way he did.

Beaten into submission by the technical jargon being drilled into them all, just to help the school show that their pupils had met expected attainment levels to improve their positions on the government's league tables.

Pressurised to write in a way that ticked boxes on data assessment sheets, following the style and format dictated to them by teachers who feared failure themselves.

Squashed - the creativity being squeezed out of them as they were forced to review, edit and rewrite the same piece of writing over and over again, banality replacing creativity, causing the pupils of George Orwell Primary to fall out of love with English and writing.

Disinterested.

Detached.

Stifled.

Fed up.

It hadn't always been like that for Zach.

He'd loved school all the way up to the end of Year 4. That was when the lower and middle schools, which shared the same school site, merged to become a single primary school with the council's move from a three-tier to two-tier school system, falling in line with the rest of the country.

Zach wouldn't have said he was the smartest of children, but he was no slouch either.

Maths was his strong suit, an aptitude for numbers being his gift. Maths was logical, it made sense.

English, on the other hand, was a different matter. It was something Zach had always had to work at as it just didn't come naturally to him.

He could read well enough, but writing, now that was a whole different kettle of fish.

Spelling and grammar didn't come easily to Zach either, to him, it was like learning a foreign language. Of course, living on a council estate in St. Godrics on the Bedfordshire/Cambridgeshire/Hertfordshire border didn't help.

Originally a quaint little market town named after the monk who tried to stop its river flooding – sadly, to no avail – St Godrics' handy proximity to London proved to be very attractive to single people and families in the late seventies/early eighties.

That, and having a train station where you could be in the capital within 30 minutes, meaning that it was a prime location for those wanting cheaper housing whilst earning above-average incomes, legally or by other less honest means, when commuting to and from London.

As St Godrics began to expand geographically, so too did its cultural diversity, with languages and accents becoming as varied and colourful as the town's lush countryside had once been.

Alas, all St Godrics now had to show for the town it once was was the statue of the brave, but foolhardy, monk St Godric himself in the old town square, crafted out of bronze, showing only the top of his head above the water with two outstretched arms holding the sheep he had rescued before being swept away by the Little Ouse River.

The town's proud home counties accent - clipped, rich and melodious - had now been replaced by a *mockney* concoction of dialects where letters, most commonly *h* and *t*, were treated with contempt, dropped, ignored and redundant in a society where slang and text-speak were now its king and queen.

Yet despite his own difficulties with his mother-tongue, Zach had looked forward to staying with the class he had been a part of since Foundation.

But his time in Year 5 and now in Year 6 had been blighted by the new teachers who had been employed to take on the extra year groups created, led by Miss Fletcher, who had also assumed the deputy head position, caused by the addition of 180 pupils who now occupied Upper Key Stage 2.

Originally with the middle school, Miss Fletcher and

three other colleagues had made the transition into primary, whilst the rest of the former middle school staff either took early retirement or had been reemployed in the schools which made up the rest of the academy federation that George Orwell Primary was now a reluctant part of.

Zach and his friends were told during their first assembly as Year 5 by Mrs Lonence, the headteacher, that these new teachers were there to 'share their vast experience and to enrich and enhance the learning of all our pupils.'

"What a load of guff," Zach muttered under his breath, partly at the memory of the lie told, but mainly at yet another instruction as to what he was supposed to include in his writing that lesson.

"I'm sorry if you think that, Zachariah," Miss Fletcher suddenly said, jolting Zach from his daydream – or was it a nightmare?

"What?"

"I said that I'm sorry that you think that my lesson is *'guff'*, as you so quaintly put it!"

"I…I…" Zach stuttered, suddenly realising that he may have spoken his private thoughts aloud, his friends' faces as they looked at him, confirmed his worse fears. "I dint mean it."

"It's *didn't,*" Miss Fletcher corrected, "And I think you most definitely did, Master Turner. I have had just about enough of your insubordination."

"Ya what?"

Miss Fletcher rolled her eyes and shook her head. "Perhaps a spell in detention at lunchtime will afford you the opportunity to reflect on your words and actions."

So it was that Zach, along with five other pupils from Year 6, soon found himself sorting, repairing and re-ordering books alphabetically in the vast library that George Orwell Primary had inherited when taking on the old middle school premises.

Fortunately for Zach, his fellow detainees happened to be some of his closest friends in school. He smiled at the irony – those ordered to spend their lunch hour amongst the books were those that had suffered most from the arrival of Miss Fletcher and her out-of-date, old-fashioned English teaching methods.

"Ya fink yoos got it bad, dude," Dev Panesar said, grappling with an impossibly large book which had been forced backwards into the bookshelf, "I got Fletch for Maths which is mental!"

"Well, least we only get her once a day," Zach laughed.

"Count yerself lucky, man," Chelsea-May replied sadly, "She job shares in our class two afternoons a week with Miss Schofield! Three whole hours at a time!"

"Yeah," Antonio added, "Ya fink it's bad her teaching ya English, try 'aving her teach French an' all!"

"How can that be worse? At least in French they don't bang on about fronted adverbials and all that other useless tosh!"

Antonio frowned as he shuffled a pile of books that were stacked on the floor before him. "Ya wouldn't fink so, would ya?"

Zach shook his head as Antonio continued, "So what's your French name then, Zach?"

"Henri."

"Henri, dat's the French version of Zach, right?"
Zach nodded, unsure as to where the conversation was heading.

"So, in our class, Paul is called *Jean-Paul*, Peter translates to *Pierre* and Amy's known as *Aimée*," Antonio said, "Even Ocean has her own French name – *Océane*."

Zach was confused. "I'm sorry dude, I still don't follow. Don't ya have a French name? Is dat what's vexing ya?"

Suddenly, Shannon, who had been quietly getting on with stacking some damaged books on the trolley beside her, laughed loudly, provoking a stern look from Mrs Yellard. "That's just it," Shannon sniggered, "He does, don't ya?"

"Don't push it!" Antonio snarled, shooting a fierce glance in Shannon's direction.

Zach looked at Shannon, then back to Antonio. "Sorry, I still don't get it."

"Whaddya fink Antonio's name is gonna be in French then?" Kadija asked, biting her lip to stem the laughter that was threatening to erupt from her face.

Zach shrugged his shoulders. "Dunno...*Antoine?*"

"Not bad," Shannon whispered as she began to wheel her trolley away, "But not right either. Go on, put him out of his misery, Antonio."

Zach looked at Antonio, who shrugged his shoulders. "It's *Bernard*."

"Ya what?"

"*Bernard*, but she says it all funny like," moaned Antonio before imitating Miss Fletcher's voice perfectly, "'Bonjour *Bernaaaaaard!*'"

Zach looked stunned as his friends, Antonio

excluded, fell into fits of laughter around him, causing Mrs Yellard to prise her ample body out of her wheelie-chair as she began to lumber in their direction.

"She really don't like ya, does she?" Zach whispered before the huge frame of the librarian loomed over them all, momentarily blocking out the watery sun that weakly shone through the dirty library windows. "Enough of this, you're not here to enjoy yourselves!" the librarian hissed.

That pretty much sums this school up, Zach thought as Mrs Yellard began to lay down the law.

"If these books are not sorted, repaired and restocked by the end of this lunch hour," she panted, the exertion from speaking seemingly too much of an effort for her oversized body, "Then I have it on Miss Fletcher's authority that you are all to return here tomorrow lunchtime, and every lunchtime after that, until the task has been done to my satisfaction."

The children looked at the masses of books which had been displaced from the shelves and randomly stacked around the library, suddenly realising that today's detention was no one-off and that Miss Fletcher had planned an extended period of punishment for their recent transgressions.

"Fat chance of that," Zach muttered, suddenly realising that the portly librarian might take further offence at the ironic comment.

Fortunately, Mrs Yellard had already turned away from them, awkwardly manoeuvring her sizeable bottom around her desk as inelegantly as a cruise liner captain docking his super-sized vessel into a tiny fishing harbour.

"It aint right, bro," Dev whinged, "They can't do dat to us. We should complain to our parents…"

Which is precisely what Zach did when he got home that night, bending the ear of, first, his mum and then his dad almost as soon as either one of them had returned from work, but only after first complaining to Emma, his annoying older sister.

As expected, the sixteen-year-old had little sympathy for her brother, simply saying, "Make the most of it, you wait 'til you get to Year 11."

Surprisingly, Zach received little encouragement from his parents for his supposed injustice either.

"You bring it on yourself, boy," his dad said in between mouthfuls at the dinner table, "I've said before, and I'll say it again, that mouth of yours will get you into trouble one of these days. Don't say I didn't warn you."

"But I dint do anyfink wrong, Dad," Zach protested, "She just don't like me 'cos I don't talk funny like her. She's always 'aving a go at me."

Zach's mum smiled sympathetically. "She's only trying to improve your English, Zach."

"My English is OK as it is, ta."

"I mean for when you leave school."

"How is talking an' writing all posh-like gonna help me? I'm gonna be a football player. Or a *YouTuber*, innit!"

Zach's parents looked at one another silently and rolled their eyes as they continued eating.

"What's wrong with dat?" Zach urged.

"Do you think that me and your mum both wanted to work in a silicon factory when we were your age?"

Zach shrugged his shoulders as he bit the end off another sausage, causing his headphone-wearing, vegan sister to wince as she tucked into her cardboard-looking nut-cutlet.

"Your dad's right, Zach," his mum nodded, "The wafer fab was the only place in town when we left school that took anyone on without having either English or Maths as a qualification. But that was over twenty years ago."

"The thing is, son," Zach's dad added, pushing his chair away from the table, walking to the sink with his now empty plate, "Without having some decent qualifications, especially English, you won't get anywhere nowadays."

"But like I said, I already talk proper, so why do I need to write stuff the way she wants me to, like?"

"Because, dummy," Emma suddenly interrupted, "If you can't fill in an application form, or write and punctuate a letter of introduction correctly, you won't get an interview for any job in the first place."

"And besides," Zach's dad said, "Even footballers and YouTubers need to know how to read, write and speak properly…"

Chapter 2

So it was that the following day Zach returned to school filled with a new sense of purpose and determination – he would try his hardest in both his Grammar and English lessons, taught consecutively by Miss Fletcher, who oversaw the Year 6, Set 2 English group.

At first, she seemed surprised and impressed with Zach's new-found enthusiasm, his hand always raised, ready to offer a reply to her questions.

But the quality of his replies and the way he conveyed them impressed her less, so, more often than not, Zach was left with his hand hanging in the air as Miss Fletcher sought a response from those pupils she deemed as more reliable and dependable.

To make matters worse, when Zach presented his independent written work to her at the end of the morning, she promptly tore it apart, verbally of course, though judging by the look on her face, if she could have physically ripped out the pages, she would have done so too...

"No subordinate conjunction fronting the adverbial clause...incorrect use of inverted commas...confused use..."

"...of the active voice," Zach repeated to Chelsea-May as he slammed another book onto the shelf.

"Man, she was well-harsh on ya!" his friend replied.

"Yep! I nearly answered her with a short *simple* sentence dat I could have *compounded* her ass with!" Zach hissed, "But it might have made my school situation even more *complex*!"

"Yo, dude!" Antonio called from the other side of the bookcase, "Dat be the most technical I ever heard ya talk about English, Ya feel me?"

"I aint gonna feel ya anytime soon, bro!" Zach replied, his anger momentarily subsiding, "It's not right though, innit?"

Chelsea-May nodded. "She a grammar-Nazi, least that's what my nan said last night."

"I fink it's probably 'cos she's so old and bitter," mumbled Shannon, her voice obscured by the large bookcase she was stood behind, "She's gotta be at least forty, right?"

"Man, that's well-old!" Zach replied, his arms now buckling under the weight of the books Chelsea-May was stacking onto them. Normally, they'd had had to carry a few books at a time by hand or use one of the library trollies. But as they had been left alone and unattended, they decided that what Mrs Yellard didn't know wouldn't hurt her.

The librarian had had to *'pop out for a couple of minutes'*, as she so quaintly put it, which the children knew was her way of saying that she was popping outside for a crafty cigarette.

This meant that they had at least fifteen minutes from when Mrs Yellard waddled off to make the slow walk out of school and into the adjoining park, ensuring that she wasn't on school property when she sparked what would undoubtedly be one *'death-stick'*, quickly followed by another.

Free from the ever-watchful librarian's beady eyes, Zach and the others had started to move books much more swiftly, throwing them to one another, or piling them up in each other's arms as Zach was doing –

Leaning-Tower-of-Pisa style – or trolley surfing, books scattering wildly as Kadija hurtled across the library floor.

After ten minutes of blissfully, pure freedom, the children reeled their activities in and returned to their previous positions, aware that the lumbering mess of a woman was bound to return at any moment.

As Zach proudly looked at the perfectly arranged bookshelf in front of him, Shannon let out an excited squeal.

"Guys, ya all gotta come and have a butcher's at the section of books I've just come across, tucked away in the corner, like!

Zach sprang from where he sat, cross-legged, on the floor and followed Chelsea-May, Dev and Kadija to where Shannon and Antonio now stood, hidden, in the furthest reaches of the library.

"Wow!" Zach said as his eyes fell on the large sign emblazoned on the front of the dark, wooden bookcase before them.

"Books They Tried to Ban," Dev read as they looked at the number of different titles tightly packed on its shelves.

"'*The Catcher in the Rye, Canterbury Tales, The Complete Tales by the Brothers Grimm,*" Zach said disappointedly, "Yeah, they sound well-gripping - not!"

"Not them - them!" Shannon repeated, pointing to another section of books, all well-read first editions, judging by the condition of their spines, age and heavy-handed readers being responsible for the poor state of them.

"Call of the Wild," Kadija read, "I've heard of that

one."

"Me too," Antonio added, "And there's a couple here by dat George Orwell bloke dat the school's named after."

"He wrote books and built schools?" Dev asked.

"Looks like it," Antonio noted, "They sound well-boring though - *1984* and *Animal Farm* - thrilling, I don't fink!"

"Dullski," yawned Chelsea-May, pulling out a book that had long lost its spine, "No way!"

"What-way?" Zach asked, shuffling closer to get a peak of the antique cover. Chelsea-May held the book up for all to see.

"*Alice's Adventures in Wonderland?*" Zach asked, "Why'd they want to ban dat?

"Dunno," Antonio shrugged, "But there are more books dat we know here – *The Witches by Roald Dahl, The Wonderful Wizard of Oz-*"

"That was a book?" Kadija asked, making to grab it from the shelf, "I have to watch that film every Christmas with me granny. Them flying monkeys scare the bejesus out of us every time!"

As she roughly pulled out the book, something dropped down from above it, before tumbling off the shelf and falling, Shannon narrowly missed catching it before it landed on the hard, wooden floor.

"They all seem pretty lame to me," Zach said yawning, "Ooh, how rad! '*Let's ban books with mad hatters, munchkins and witches who hate children!'*"

"Sounds like Miss Fletcher, Mrs Guthrie and Miss Francis, dat!" laughed Kadija.

"Yep, Francis is almost as bad, but at least she's a lot fitter than them other two."

"Get you!" laughed Antonio, "Me man Zach's got himself a crush on *Fancy* Francis!"

"Shut ya mouth or I'm gonna shut it for ya!"

"Make me!"

Nobody noticed Shannon's face as the two boys squared up to one another. If they had then they'd have noticed a grin almost as wide as the Cheshire cat's soon crack across her pretty features.

"Hey, guys, cut it out! Ya gotta be seeing this."

Kadija, Chelsea-May and Dev turned toward Shannon, their short attention spans needing no second invitation to lose interest in the two boys who pouted and posed opposite one another, before falling to the floor in fits of laughter.

"Come on, *Bernaaaard,*" laughed Zach, putting an arm around Antonio's shoulders, "Let's see what Shannon's found now, dude."

"Probably an X-rated version of *The Tale of Mrs.Tiggy-Winkle,*" Antonio replied as they quickly joined the scrum now gathered around Shannon.

"What ya got there," Zach asked, trying to peer through the melee of arms and heads before him, "It better be good, like."

"Oh, I fink it is," Shannon smiled as she thrust the thick, red leather-bound book she held in front of his face, so close to Zach's nose that he had to take a step back for his eyes to be able to fully focus on it.

But once they had, Zach gasped as its title and the implications it had for him and his friends slowly began to sink in.

"*Grammarticus,*" Zach mumbled the book's title, his voice raising as he read aloud the subtitle beneath it, "*How to Make Your English Truly Magical.*"

"It's just another of dem damned exercise books dat Fletch and dem others make us work from, innit?" Dev moaned, disappointedly.

"Nah, dude," Shannon said, flipping open the cover, the book seeming to sigh as she did so, "This seems different. Look."

The children gathered around Shannon as she struggled to lay the book on the floor. Zach noticed that its pages were crisp and yellow, weathered by the passage of time.

"See this," Shannon insisted, pointing to the bold, cursive text, "It's been hand-written."

"All books are hand-written, Shan," Kadija sniffed sarcastically, "How else do writers write dem?"

Shannon rolled her eyes and was about to answer when Zach butted in. "She's right, Kadge. It aint been printed like books are nowadays. Dis one has been written with one of dem fancy pens."

"What, *Berols*?" Antonio asked.

Zach shook his head. "Nah, the ones dat have a pointy bit, like a knife, dat the ink comes out of. Me grandad has one. Now, what's it called again…it's something to do with water…"

The children stood there momentarily before Chelsea-May shouted, "Got it – a jelly pen!"

"Ya mean a *gel* pen, dummy," Dev sneered, "Anyway, what's jelly got to do with water?"

"Me nan uses boiling water to make it," Chelsea-May sniffed, sulkily.

Zach scratched his head before announcing excitedly. "Fountain pen! Dat's it! All the oldies used to use dem when they were at school."

"Now that's sorted, can we get back to what it says,"

Shannon sighed as she too read the text aloud,
"'*Grammarticus by Elrond Hubbard: How to Make
Your English Truly Magical-*'"
"We know dat, it says so on the cover," Antonio
sighed, "What else does it say?"
"Keep your hair on, Ant," Shannon replied, "I was
just getting to dat. She ran her finger under the text
and continued to read the next line of spidery writing,
"'*Editor's Note: Warning - The contents of this book
will change the reader's life forever. Only those
schooled in the dark art of word are permitted to
incant the scripture written or use and share the
knowledge shared within the pages of this tome-*'"
"Ya what?" Antonio said, "None of dat gubbins
makes any sense, like."
"Shut it, Ant," Zach said, jabbing Antonio in the ribs,
"Go on, Shan."
Shannon nodded and made to turn the page but froze
at the hacking, coughing sound which broke the
silence around them."
"Quick, *Yellers* coming back!" Kadija urged as the
heavy sound of footsteps began to echo through the
library as the overweight librarian wheezed her way
back into the room.
Shannon slammed the cover shut and shoved the
mysterious book back onto the shelf as the rest of the
children scuttled to the positions that Mrs Yellard had
left them in earlier that lunchtime.
"I see that you've made *some* progress," Mrs Yellard
huffed as she looked at the pile of books which,
although diminished, still required further sorting,
repairing and stacking, "But it looks like you guys
will be back here again tomorrow."

An audible groan filled the library as Mrs Yellard continued, "And judging by your current rate of progress, or lack of it, you'll be straight back here after the weekend too."

Chapter 3

Any curiosity that the six children may have had about the strange leather-bound book they'd just discovered soon disappeared once they'd left the library, their short-attention spans moving on to more pressing matters, such as that afternoon's PE lessons and what they'd respectively have to eat later that evening.

It was only when Zach sat with his sister and parents at dinner as they'd interrogated him about his day, that the strange book he and his friends had briefly come across began to enter his thoughts once more.

"How's lunchtime detention going, bro?" Emma had asked, deliberately snatching a particularly juicy slice of pizza away from Zach's grasp.

"You still on detention?" his mum repeated as Zach sank in his chair, crossing his arms sulkily.

"Less of that," Zach's dad said as he frowned at his son, "There's plenty enough to go around. Now, don't be rude - answer your mum."

"Sorry, Dad," Zach replied, grabbing another slice of the pizza, sticking his pepperoni-covered tongue out at his sister as he did so.

"Well?"

"Well, what?

Zach's mum shook her head, "The library detention – you still having to attend them?"

"Yeah, we're still in there," Zach mumbled, his tongue now lassoing a slippery piece of mozzarella which was threatening to escape the prison of his mouth, "Talk about *Dullsville*. Nothing but books, books and more books all lunchtime, every day this week!"

"That's what you get if you mess with the teachers, son," his dad replied, unsympathetically, "Look on the bright side, maybe having to spend that amount of time in a library might convince you to read a little more often. You don't read anywhere near enough."

"No way," Zach replied, "Give me YouTube any day!"

"*'Books are a uniquely portable magic,'*" Emma said, smugly, "At least that's what Mr King himself says."

"Is that one of your teachers, Em?" Zach's mum asked, causing Zach to almost choke on his pizza.

"Mum! Even I know dat she's talking 'bout *Stephen King*, the author!" Zach grinned, as his mum flushed bright red. He was about to continue but the mention of *'magic'* had flicked a light-switch on in his head. His dad immediately noticed the stranger-than-usual look on his son's face. "Come on, spit it out."

"What? Me pizza?"

"No dude, what you were thinking. If it was something rude about your mum…"

"It aint nothing to do with Mum," Zach said, hesitantly.

"Well," his dad insisted, "What then?"

"I was just finking 'bout this book we came across today, right. It was well-old."

"Some books are, dummy," Emma said, adding, "They were here way before the internet was."

"Em, you're not helping," her mum said, "Go on, Zach."

"Like I was saying, this book was well-ancient, like years old. So old, in fact, dat it looked like it had been hand-written, ya know what I mean?"

"What was it called?" Zach's dad asked.

Zach shrugged his shoulders. "Sumfink to do with grammar, don't remember what though."

"Sounds about right,"

"Emma!"

"Sorry, Dad!"

"What *can* you remember about it, Zach?"

Zach frowned. "It had a red, leather cover, yellow pages, smelt a bit like cat-wee, and was written by some geezer called Elrond summat-or-other."

His mum frowned. "Are you sure?"

Zach nodded. "Yeah, totes. Elrond, like the name of dat elf out of dat film…er…*Lord of Dem Fings* or summat!"

Zach's dad shot his mum a concerned look

"What? What?" Zach asked

"Was it Elrond *Hubbard*?" his dad asked.

"Dat's it! Ya know him?"

"Oh yes," Zach's mum frowned, "Everybody our age knows all about Mr Hubbard. He was our old headmaster for a while."

Zach wasn't quite sure what the exchanged glances between his parents meant but he pressed on with his question anyway. "He a good headteacher?"

"Totally!" his dad replied, "All of the kids loved him, unless he jangled his keys in his pocket. Then you stayed well-clear of him and his temper."

"Some said that he could be a mean and nasty man if you got the wrong side of him," Zach's mum added, "And that he had his favourites. I never saw that myself, but if it was true, then it undoubtedly contributed greatly to his downfall, ultimately being

27

the end of him at George Orwell."

Zach immediately picked up on the ominous tone his mum used when talking about Elrond Hubbard. "Whaddya mean, the *'end of him'*? Did he die or summat?"

Zach's dad laughed. "Course not, Mr Hubbard may still be alive and kicking for all we know! No, what your mum meant was because he had his favourites, especially the school governors' children, that soon spelt the end of his school career."

Zach listened intently as his dad explained how Mr Hubbard seemed to have an uncanny knack of taking the most unlikely of students and managed to get them through the dreaded 11+ exams, guaranteeing them a place at the much sought-after grammar school nearby.

"Usually they weren't even the brightest of kids," Zach's mum said sadly.

Her husband nodded his head in agreement. "That's right, they definitely weren't the sharpest tools in the shed! But their families had money to burn, so their futures were guaranteed, unlike the likes of me and your mum."

"I still don't geddit," sighed Zach, "If they weren't the smartest, then surely no amount of dosh would help dem pass?"

Again, his parents looked at one another, apparently weighing up as to what to say next.

It was left to Emma to fill in the blanks. "You don't need to be smart to pass some exams; you just need to know the answers before taking them!"

"But dat's cheating, innit?"

"Yes, it is," Zach's dad agreed, "But the fact was that

children, no better at English and Maths than me or your mum were suddenly getting scores that made them look like geniuses. They sailed through their exams and made it onto *Easy Street* with no real effort at all."

"It was only after Taylor Smith supposedly snitched that the governors suspended Mr Hubbard whilst they carried out a full investigation."

Zach's head was spinning. "Why'd he snitch?"

"No one knows for certain," his mum replied, "They are a lot of myths and rumours which surround that time. But the one I heard was that Taylor cottoned on to what was going on and tried to blackmail Mr Hubbard into giving him the exam answers for free."

"When he didn't," his dad added, "Then Taylor allegedly spilt the beans and told the chair of governors who had no children at the school herself."

Zach imagined how the events must have unfolded as his dad continued to explain how Mr Hubbard had denied any wrong-doing and that all of the excellent results had been achieved through extra-curricular-lessons he'd taught privately, outside of his normal school hours.

It was only when his dad began to recount how those who'd been given additional tuition by Hubbard had claimed that they hadn't paid for any answers and that they had passed the exam fairly and squarely that Zach spoke again.

"Did they say what it was dat made Hubbard's tuition work so well?"

"A book," Zach's mum answered, "They claimed a lightbulb *'just sparked'* in their heads when they worked from the journals that Mr Hubbard had written especially for them."

"That's right," Zach's dad added, "So, if it had only been Taylor's word against that of Mr Hubbard and the other pupils, then that would have been that as there was no other proof against him. Except…"

Again, that knowing look between his parents.

"'Cept *what*?" Zach urged.

As his dad revealed to him that just a few days later, under a full moon, Mr Hubbard was supposedly caught making a *blood-sacrifice* behind the school bike sheds, Zach felt his stomach twist into knots.

"Mr Hubbard claimed that he was trying to save a rabbit, or something, that had been attacked by a fox," Zach's dad said, shaking his head, "No one believed him of course, but rather than go to court and cause an even bigger scandal, Mr Hubbard suddenly *'retired'*. He supposedly left town soon after, we've not seen or heard of him since."

"Coincidently, the passes for the 11+ started to drop pretty soon after that," Zach's mum added.

Zach felt as though he'd been hit by a sledgehammer as his dad drained his glass before looking him straight in the eye again.

"Take my advice, Zach. If that book you found is by Elrond Hubbard, then stay well clear of it - don't touch it with a bargepole, you hear me?"

"Yes, Dad."

Normally that would have been it.
Dad had spoken.
End of discussion.
No questions asked.
Matter closed.

'*Move along now, there's nothing to see here*,' type of thing.

Usually, when his dad told him not to do something, then Zach would obey, whether he agreed with it or not.

Dad's word was law.

Zach fully intended to abide by it and have nothing to do with Hubbard's book ever again when he arrived at school that fateful Friday morning.

That was until after morning break.

Until lesson 2.

Until English.

Until the F Word - *Fletcher*!

"This is unacceptable gibberish," she ranted, her shrill, nasally voice making eyes bleed, set teeth on edge and possibly sent all the dogs in the local neighbourhood running for cover, as she tottered around the classroom, the luscious, long, auburn wig she so obviously wore threatening to detach itself from her head, such was her rage and anger.

Miss Fletcher began to toss exercise books back and forth across the room, venomously spitting her fury at their owners as each one landed in front of its hapless victim.

"Dull…insipid…poor use of standard English… tedious…no fronted adverbials… no embedded clauses…incorrect tense use… confused use of active and passive verbs…mixed narrative voice…"

And as each book slapped the table surface in front of its owner, Zach's stomach tightened as he waited for his English book to be thrown toward him whilst Miss Fletcher continued her verbal assault on the class.

But, surprisingly, it was not forthcoming as Miss Fletcher suddenly stopped at the front of the room, one blue-covered exercise book still held in her scrawny, liver-spotted, age-weathered hands.

"All of you have something that you need to work on should you have even the faintest chance of passing your SATs tests," she sneered, turning her eyes toward Zach, "But you, Master Turner, you have even surpassed yourself this time! Your English skills, or should I say, lack of them, take you onto an entirely different level of ineptitude and incompetence."

Zach ducked as the missile-like exercise book came hurtling toward him, shaving yet more hair off his closely cropped scalp. He bent down to retrieve the book from where it lay behind him as Miss Fletcher sighed and sat on the edge of her desk, to glare as the shell-shocked children gathered in front of her.

"In almost thirty years of teaching," she said, her voice calming slightly, "I have never come across such a careless attitude towards the use of the English language. So, starting Monday, we will dedicate all our lessons to learning how to pass the SATs tests."

The class groaned as she stood and made her way to the wipe board behind her and began to furiously scribble on it.

"However, if your name is on the board, you will also be expected to come in during your lunchtimes for extra tuition and revision."

Zach rolled his eyes as he saw his name top the list, closely followed by those of Shannon and Kadija, who shook their heads in front of him, along with the names of Dev, Antonio and Chelsea-May, amongst others.

Shannon quickly raised a hand. "Miss?"

"Yes, Shannon," Miss Fletcher replied sharply without turning.

"If extra English revision is starting next week during lunchtimes, we won't be able to make it."

Miss Fletcher turned and scowled. "And why, may I ask, is that?"

"Because we're still sorting out the library."

Miss Fletcher smiled, not the nice type of smile sweet old people like your grandparents make.

No, this was more like the smile of an elderly person who hated the fact that youth was still the prize of the stupid.

"Then I suggest you hurry up and finish it then, dear," she said, sarcastically, "Otherwise it'll be Easter school for you."

Chapter 4

"Dey can't do dat, can dey?" Antonio asked as he and the others met again in the library that lunchtime. They had waited until Mrs Yellard had gone for her usual *'walk'* before talking about the events of the morning.

"They can," Shannon replied sadly, "Fletcher said they are 'aving extra SATs mornings and it'll be compulsory for those picked."

"Fancy Francis said the same to our English set today," Chelsea-May said sadly.

"Dat aint right, surely dey can't do dat?" Dev asked. Shannon shrugged her shoulders. "They're panicking about SATs, so they'll do whatever they can to make the school look good, then blame us for being too fick if we don't pass."

"Maybe our parents will say no to extra stuff during the holidays," Dev asked hopefully.

Chelsea-May shook her head. "If they're anyfink like mine, they'll likely bite their hands off. Free child-care during the school holidays, aint it, Zach?"

Zach didn't reply. He just sat, cross-legged on the floor, staring at the imposing bookcase directly in front of him.

"Zach," Chelsea-May repeated, "Ya OK?"

"Huh?" answered Zach, seeming to snap out of the spell that he appeared to be under, "Sorry, what'd you say?"

Shannon smiled. "We were talking 'bout the extra grammar lessons and Easter school the teachers said we gotta do."

"Oh dat," Zach replied, quickly getting to his feet

before walking briskly towards one of the bookcases, "I aint doing it."

Shannon looked at the others who shrugged their shoulders back at her. "I don't fink we've gotta choice."

Zach paused for a moment and pinched the end of his nose briefly, something he always did when he was deciding something. "Shan, there's always a choice," he replied, his decision seemingly made as he bent down and reached behind the row of books haphazardly lined up on the bottom shelf.

He rummaged around for a moment until his hand rested on the cracked leather cover of the book his dad had warned him to steer clear of. "There ya go!" Antonio watched as Zach struggled to pull the heavy tome from the shelf.

"Fink he's lost it," Antonio said, twirling a finger around his temple as if to further illustrate the point.

Zach lifted the book high and slammed it onto one of the reading desks nearby, switching a small light on to illuminate the cover once more.

"Grammarticus," he whispered as he opened the cover and started to turn its pages as his friends began to crowd around him.

"Ya picked a fine time to decide to read that fing, Zach," Kadija said as she watched him carefully run a finger under the text he was now reading.

"Yeah, Zach," agreed Dev, "Why the sudden interest in it?"

"No time to go into all the detail," Zach said, "But if me dad is right, then this book is all we need to sort our English problems once an' for all, ya feel me?"

Antonio repeated the gesture with his finger as Dev,

Shannon, Kadija and Chelsea-May all stared at each other blankly.

"Trust me," Zach said as he began to read the book's foreword, written by Elron Hubbard himself,

"*'English is the most beautiful, but difficult, language in the world to master, an almost uncontrollable beast...'*"

As Zac continued to hesitantly read the page, his friends began to yawn and grow restless, all too aware that Yellard would soon be back to make their lives a living hell once again.

"Blimey, this is even more boring than listening to Fletcher drone on," Shannon yawned, "C'mon we've got work to do-"

"Knew it! Zach laughed, jabbing a page in the book, "Got ya!"

"What...what?" Antonio asked.

Zach raised his head and grinned at his friends. "This aint no ordinary textbook. Listen to this..."

The children drew closer around him as Zach began to carefully read the words that would change their lives forever.

"*'I have dedicated my life to finding the secrets of our magnificent mother-tongue,'*" Hubbard's writing seemed to come alive as Zach spoke them, "*'Years spent learning their rhythms and patterns, becoming a master of the dark art of word, lacing this book with translations of lost spells and incantations to help those who find they are unable to naturally rise above their given station, cursed by the inability to speak perfectly in their native lang-'*"

"Glad you're reading this, dude," Dev said, "I ain't got a clue what the hell this geezer's going on about!"

Zach shrugged his shoulders. "Me neither, but if this book really got all them other students through their exams, then dat's good enough for me, innit?"

Zach skim read the rest of the page until he reached the last sentence. *"'So, dear reader, good luck in your quest for knowledge. But remember, you too must master the dark art of word before using any of the spells in this book."*

"Spells?" Shannon gasped, "Ya telling me dat this is some sort of *magic* book."

Zach laughed. "Don't be stupid, Shan! Magic don't exist, do it? It's obviously a typo, a mistake. He probably meant spellings."

Shannon frowned. "Then what does the geezer mean when he says dat ya have to have mastered the dark art of word?"

"Umm," Zach said uncertainly, before his face brightened, "It's probably what WordArt was called when it first came out, innit? And anyone will tell ya dat I am a whizz with it in Computing, ya know what I mean?"

With that, Zach excitedly turned to Chapter 1, squinting at what appeared to be tiny black marks which totally covered one of the pages.

However, on closer inspection, he noticed that one of the marks appeared to be moving, two microscopic antennae twitching furiously above its head.

Shannon noticed this too as, slowly but surely, each little mark began to move across the paper, seeming to grow slightly as they did so.

"Whaddya looking at?" Antonio asked, moving round to the top of the bookstand along with the others.

This is too good to be true, Zach thought as he

lowered his head closer to the page and blew the marks, causing them to scatter all over his friends, the backdraft his breath caused meant that a couple of the strange marks covered him as well.

"Aargh! Get 'em off me!" Dev shrieked, swatting his arm.

"Ya wuss," laughed Chelsea-May as she casually stroked her arm, "It's only dust."

"I'm not so sure," Shannon replied as she shook her top, the marks falling like dandruff to the ground. "These fings are definitely moving."

"Book mites," Kadija said, "Saw a show once where these books all fell apart. Them fings live on the glue that holds books together."

"Gross," Dev said, shuddering as he writhed in his clothes, imagining tiny little feet still walking over his skin. "Are there any more in dat fing?"

"Chill dude, there's just some more writing," Zach said as he continued to read, "'*Remember not only to say the right thing in the right place, but far more difficult still, to leave unsaid the wrong word at the most tempting moment.'*"

"Huh?" Dev asked, "Hubbard wrote that?"

"Don't fink so," Zach replied, "It says *based on the quote by Benjamin Franklin'* at the end of it."

"Who's he? Did he work at the school an' all?"

"Dunno."

"Fink he was an American inventor or a president, or summat like that," Kadija said.

"Looks like Hubbard liked him then," said Shannon, "What else has he written?"

Zach frowned as he struggled to decode the next sentence. "Just this - *Eloquencius, Loquacious.*"

"That's well-weird," Antonio said, "Does it say what it means?"

Zach shook his head.

"What else it say?" Kadija asked, struggling to look at the page.

"Nuffink," Zach replied, flicking over a dozen blank pages, "Dat's the end of this chapter."

"Odd," Shannon said as Zach slammed the book shut.

"Exactly," Dev replied and was about to continue, but the sound of the heavy, fire doors which led into the library being flung open caused the six children to scatter in all directions, Zach quickly inserting *Grammarticus* back into its previous location in the bookcase.

"Haven't you lot finished yet?" Mrs Yellard yawned, "I'll be drawing my school pension by the time the six of you are done!"

"Begging your pardon, Mrs Yellard," Antonio said, popping his head out from behind the bookcase that hid him, "We are doing our absolute best. On behalf of my fellow students, please accept my most humble apologies for our tardiness this fine afternoon."

It was hard to fathom whose mouth had fallen open the furthest – Mrs Yellard's or the rest of the children who now stood, staring at Antonio who frowned back at them.

"Oh dear? Have I transgressed? Did I say the wrong thing?"

"Quite the opposite, Master Dalla Bona," Mrs Yellard replied, hauling herself up out of her swivel chair, "I don't think I have ever heard you speak so eloquently and beautifully."

Antonio glared back at the old librarian. "Please

forgive me for asking, but are you being sarcastic, my good lady?"

Before Mrs Yellard could respond, the school bell rang signalling the end of lunch.

"Come along now, Antonio," Zach said, grabbing his friend by the arm, "Time for us to depart, post-haste. Good afternoon, Mrs Yellard."

The librarian stood, mouth agape, as Zach quickly led Antonio out through the library doors, closely followed by the rest of their friends.

They had hardly walked 100 metres before Antonio abruptly stopped, wrenching his arm from Zach's grasp.

"I must strongly protest at you manhandling me so," Antonio said angrily, "Especially as Mrs Yellard was mocking me in such an unkind manner."

"My dear, Antonio," Zach said calmly, "She wasn't mocking you. You really did speak to her in the most splendid of ways."

Antonio stared at Zach. "May I ask, what is wrong with you?"

"Absolutely nothing, my dear fellow. Pray tell, why do you ask?"

"Perhaps it's because it sounds as though one's swallowed a dictionary!"

The two friends glared at one another; the uncomfortable silence only broken by the laughter that soon echoed around them.

"And what, may I enquire most urgently," Zach said angrily, turning to look at Shannon and the others, "Do you all find so highly amusing?"

"Oh, how very *lah-di-dah!*" Shannon laughed, "Now, let me see…Maybe it's because the pair of you sound as though you've just stepped off the set of one of those *ever-so-posh* television shows that one watches, such as *Downton Abbey*!"

Antonio looked confused. "Would you care to elaborate further?"

That proved to be too much for Kadija and Chelsea-May who fell about on the floor, Dev also struggling to contain himself beside them.

"A most excellent jape, my dear boys," Shannon chuckled, "As much as one would like to chat about this with you, we've further lessons to attend. See you both again on Monday. Good day."

Antonio and Zach stood and watched as their friends raced down the corridor, dodging in and out of the other pupils who were hurriedly making their way back to their classes.

"Please tell me," Antonio finally said, "Is it just oneself, or did Shannon's voice and accent sound most peculiar when she was conversing with us…?"

Chapter 5

Zach and Antonio hardly had time to dwell on the matter that afternoon as, first, they had had to take part in a number of circuit activities in PE, which left them unable to breathe, let alone speak.

Then there was Key Stage 2 Club time in the media suite, both boys totally immersed in the coding club activities that they took part in.

In fact, it wasn't until Zach had slumped on his sofa, having walked home alone after school, that his thoughts again turned back to that lunchtime.

I must admit, Zach thought as he watched some over-cheerful, white-toothed presenter laugh incessantly on the television, *how Antonio spoke to Mrs Yellard today was frightfully entertaining.* Zach paused the TV. *Frightfully entertaining? Oh, my giddy aunt! One sounds just as bad, even when one thinks to oneself.*

He sat bolt upright before darting up the stairs to stare at himself in the bathroom mirror.

Zach's hazel-brown eyes glared back at him as he peered at his reflection.

He still looked like Zach, but there was something different about his image, something more confident about the way he now regarded himself.

My, you're such a handsome fellow, Zachariah.

There it was again, the voice in his head.

His voice, but in tone only.

However, the words, unspoken, sounded alien to him.

There was not a trace of the accent that hung on to those that lived in his town.

Nor the slang his fellow students used on a daily basis, their own language, their own dialect and secret, spoken code,

It was more like the language they were forcibly fed a daily diet of in school by Fletcher and her antiquarian colleagues.

What did they call it?

"Standard English, dear boy", Zach suddenly said, adding, "Or the Queen's English, to be more precise." In the mirror, Zach could see his mouth moving, but he didn't recognise who the words belonged to, so alien did his speech sound to him.

"What on Earth has happened to me?" Zach frowned as he recalled accusing Antonio of swallowing a dictionary.

No, Zach thought, *not a dictionary, more like a grammar encyclo-*

He suddenly stopped, mid-thought.

It couldn't be, could it?

But before he could answer himself mentally, he heard the front door slam downstairs.

"Hi hun, I'm home," he heard his mum shout cheerfully, "Come tell me all about your day, sweetheart."

"Oh, my," Zach muttered, "Won't this be all fine and dandy!"

Fumbling around in his pocket, Zach finally produced his mobile phone and, using both thumbs, began to text frantically;

'hey guys, fink we need 2 meet b4 skool monday'

Zach frowned briefly, noticing that although his speech had dramatically changed, his use of the written word showed no such improvement.

Undeterred, he continued to type;

'don't no bout you all but theres deffo sumfink diffrent bout me since reading dat book .txt me back L8Rs'

Zach added his friends to the group chat before hitting the '*SEND*' button on his phone.
"Did you hear me, Zach?" his mum called from downstairs.
"Yes, Mother, I'll be with you, post-haste!" Zach shouted, his phone vibrating repeatedly in his pocket as he raced down the stairs…

"Blimey, kids, you wet the bed or something?"
Mr Copthorne, the school site manager, laughed as he unlocked the doors to the library.
"Not quite," Zach smiled, "But one does feel somewhat jaded this fine morning."
"Oh, does one?" Mr Copthorne scoffed, "Careful, you're starting to sound like that Miss Fletcher, the stuck-up bit-" the site manager stopped, mid-sentence, as he suddenly remembered his audience before quickly changing the subject.
"And you're sure that Mrs Yellard said that it was all right for you to be here on your own?"
"Scouts' honour," Antonio smiled, holding three fingers up toward Mr Copthorne.
"That's all right then. Remember to shout if you need anything, kids."
Zach and his friends watched as the former soldier limped off, his keys, which hung from a large key chain clipped to his waistband, clanging erratically as

he did so.

"Quick," Zach said urgently as he raced to the bookcase that housed *Grammarticus,* "There's no time to dally!"

"I'm not altogether sure as to why we are all here at such a godforsaken hour," Kadija yawned as she rubbed her eyes, causing the others around her to unconsciously mimic her actions.

Zach shook his head as he moved the books that wedged *Grammarticus* into the bookcase out of the way. "As you have all noticed and commented on in your texts, we've all drastically changed the way we speak since I read from this on Friday."

Zach winced as he lifted the heavy tome and again rested it on the nearest reading stand.

"That is most true," Shannon said as Zach began to quickly rifle through the book's pages, "It has been the source of much hilarity in my household this past weekend."

"Mine too," agreed Antonio, "It's as though everything I say has been perfectly written for me."

"I concur!" Chelsea-May added excitedly, "My parents have been teasing me incessantly, asking me if I know a centaur, a talking lion and the snow queen!"

"Exactly!" Antonio nodded, "We sound as though our speech has been written by that chap who wrote all those books about Narnia."

Shannon's eyes widened. "By golly gosh, yes! I'm now a character from a C. S. Lewis novel!"

"Apologies, Shannon," Zach said, frowning as he flicked blank page after blank page, "But you sound a trifle more Mary Poppins than Lucy or Susan

Pevensie!"

Shannon held her middle finger up towards Zach. "Manners, Shannon," Kadija laughed, "That's awfully crude and unladylike!"

"It's a good job that one isn't a lady then," Shannon sneered, adding, "I have to agree with Kadija in saying that I am a little confused as to why we are here this early though. We were all due to be here at lunchtime anyway. What's the sudden urgency?"

"Since reading this, our spoken language has improved, would you not agree?" Zach asked, jabbing his finger onto yet another empty page.

Chelsea-May sighed. "We've already been through this, my dear…"

"Please, allow him to finish," Antonio pleaded, "Pray continue, my dear friend."

"Thank you," Zach said, "As I was saying, Hubbard's book has already proved itself in how we now converse. However, when I wrote my texts to you, my written English was still just as appalling."

"He's right, you know," Dev nodded, "I was having to practise my spellings with *Mater* and *Pater* last night and I still couldn't spell for toffee!"

Shannon frowned. "Am I right in thinking that we are still going to fail our mock SATs tests this week then, despite our new verbosity?"

Zach nodded, continuing to turn the pages of the books, "Yes, unless we manage to find something else, that is. Hence our early arrival here this morning."

Shannon and the others closed in around *Grammarticus* as Zach continued to turn its blank pages, growing more and more frustrated as he did so.

"I don't understand," he said, frustratingly running his fingers across his scalp, "Why so many blank pages with no writing on them?"

"Perhaps there was nothing else other than that first written spell," Kadija said sadly, "Perhaps it's yet another cruel trick played by an unkind teacher on those that are so desperate for help."

"Or perhaps," Shannon said as she began to quickly turn the pages herself, "It's a test to see how desperately we want to improve ourselves. There!" Shannon's finger triumphantly stabbed a page with the heading '*Chapter 2.*' "Go on then, Zachariah, read on."

"Why me?"

"Well, it worked for you last time," Shannon smiled, "And, besides, you're easily the best reader out all of us here!"

Zach looked at his other friends, who all nodded and smiled back at him."

"That's not saying a lot then is it?" he grinned as he began to read aloud, *"'English doesn't borrow from other languages. English follows other languages down dark alleys, knocks them over and goes through their pockets for loose vocabulary - James D. Nicoll'"*

"That's almost as bizarre as the first thing you read us, Zachariah," Antonio sighed.

Zach nodded. "There's more this time, there's a poem by some chap called James Donovan too," he cleared his throat and began to read aloud again;

"'We'll begin with box; the plural is boxes;
But the plural of ox is oxen, not oxes,

One fowl is a goose, and two are called geese,
Yet the plural of moose is never called meese.
You can find a lone mouse or a house full of mice;
But the plural of house is houses not hice.
The plural of man is always men.
But the plural of pan is never pen.
If I speak of a foot, and you show me two feet,
And I give you a book, would a pair be a beek?
If one is a tooth and a whole set are teeth,
Why shouldn't two booths be called beeth?
If the singular's this and the plural is these,
Should the plural of kiss be ever called keese?
We speak of a brother and also of brethren,
But though we say mother, we never say methren.
When the masculine pronouns are he, his, and him;
Just imagine the feminine.... she, shis, and shim!'"

"Well, that's a clear as custard, isn't it?" Shannon sighed.

"Yes," Zach said, turning the page, "There's one final paragraph in this chapter though. But it must be really important as it's been heavily underlined."

"What does it say?" Dev asked

"'*Graecorum vero - speak and write the grammar of truth, even if both your pen and voice shake.'*"

Suddenly, without warning, the lines under each word seemed to swell and grow as they reared up and flew off the page, like snakes charmed out of their baskets.

"What the…" Shannon began to say but before she could continue, the lines began to wriggle across the page.

"Oh my, they look like worms," Kadija said, "Bookworms!"

Almost immediately, the *bookworms* shot off in every direction, zooming towards each of them, disappearing just before reaching the face of each child, causing them to sneeze violently.

"It smells really musty, almost like…" Antonio began, wiping his nose with his sleeve.

"Old books," Chelsea-May completed his sentence for him. "Have we just inhaled magic worms? I've heard of earworms before, but nose-worms? That's not a *thing,* is it?

The children all looked at one another before Dev suddenly burst out laughing. "Don't talk utter nonsense! I think we're letting our imagination get the better of us here, wouldn't you say?" Dev looked at Shannon for further reassurance.

"Probably," she replied before turning to Zach. "I don't suppose you've any more surprises for us today, do you, Zach?"

Zach puffed, shook his head and closed the book. "I'm afraid not. That was the end of the second chapter."

The children looked at one another in silence for a moment or two, until Antonio plucked up the courage to speak first. "Aside from the mystery of the book worms, how will we know if the spell has worked or not?"

Zach pulled his mobile out of his pocket and began to type, instantly smiling as he did so.

Almost immediately, a chorus of ringtones echoed around the library as all of his friends fumbled to retrieve their phones.

Each one of them smiled as they read the text that Zach had sent them;

'O ye of little faith! It appears that this worm has truly turned! I, for one, have no doubt nor reservations, that Grammarticus has given us the blessed gift of perfect spoken and written grammar!
Once more, unto the breach again, dear friends, once more!'

Chapter 6

Normally, whenever Zach walked into Miss Fletcher's class for English, fear and trepidation would overwhelm him, almost drowning him in a sea of anxiety.

Not today.

Today, he entered the room in a cool, calm and confident manner, one which was immediately noted by the teacher herself.

"Has something tickled your fancy, Master Turner?"

For some reason he couldn't explain, Zach began to giggle uncontrollably, much to the bemusement of Miss Fletcher, as well as the rest of his classmates. Conscious of raising any further suspicion, Zach bit hard against the side of his cheek, something he used to do when he was younger, usually when his dad tickled him to within an inch of his life.

"My apologies, Miss Fletcher," Zach said, "I don't quite know what came over me."

Miss Fletcher stared fiercely at him. "Well, I suggest that you pull yourself together before we start the spelling test otherwise you'll be laughing on the other side of your face."

Zach sat on his hands, desperately suppressing the urge which had suddenly come over him, to grab his clothing and tug at it furiously.

"Once again, my most sincere apologies, Miss Fletcher," Zach said quietly, speaking through a small gap in the side of his mouth.

Miss Fletcher eyed him suspiciously, as though determining whether he was deliberately mocking her but, on seeing Zach open his pencil case and prepare himself for the first test, decided to give him the benefit of the doubt.

On this occasion, at least.

"Right, children," Miss Fletcher began to announce, "Today is your spelling test, which you will have twenty minutes to complete it in. Tomorrow will be Grammar and Punctuation, Wednesday Comprehension and, finally, on Thursday, I'll be giving you an unaided writing task. Questions?"

Shannon raised her hand. "I didn't think that we had an unaided activity task for SATs, Miss Fletcher."

Miss Fletcher smiled, the smile not quite reaching her eyes. "And you would be correct in thinking that," she said, moving around her desk to sit down, "However, after the shambolic pieces of writing – and I use the term *writing* loosely - you all submitted last week, I have decided to add one of my own in the vain hope that we may yet avoid having to have additional Easter classes."

"Rest assured," Zach said cheerily as the teaching assistant, Mrs Kaur, handed him his test sheet, "We shall not let you down. In fact, some of us may surprise you with our endeavours."

Miss Fletcher looked at Zach over the top of her glasses. "Trust me, Master Turner, nothing that you could ever do could possibly surprise me. Your twenty minutes begin…now!"

Zach listened intently as Miss Fletcher began to read the spellings, first saying the word, then using it in a sentence, before repeating the word a third and final time.

Normally he'd sit and struggle to decode the word that he heard said, trying to work out the correct letter pattern and spelling structure when writing each word down, sounding it out carefully.

But not today.

No, as Miss Fletcher read out the spellings, Zach would look up and somehow see the words form in the air in front of him in a serious of luminous colours, the letters seeming to vibrate, as though singing to him. He looked to see if anyone else was looking around and noticed that Shannon and Kadija appeared to be experiencing the same sensation, quickly dropping their heads again before scribbling away furiously.

Zach smiled as he placed his pen on the test paper, grinning as he watched his spidery script transform into perfectly formed cursive writing, each loop and curl a thing of beauty in its intricacy and detail.

When Miss Fletcher eventually announced that their time was up, Zach put his pen down and looked around the classroom.

Only Kadija and Shannon had the same look of contentment on their faces, they too having completed the spelling test with ease.

Grammarticus works, Zach thought as Mrs Kaur collected their sheets, smiling warmly as she looked at Zach's perfectly presented paper.

"Well done, Zach," she whispered, winking at him as she passed, "Let's hope that the others have done as well as you!"

Oh, I am most certain that there will be five of my peers who are feeling as confident as I do now, Zach thought, smiling.

And so it proved to be the case when he, Shannon and Kadija met Dev, Antonio and Chelsea-May in the library that lunchtime.

"That was a most splendid test today," Antonio grinned, slapping Zach squarely on the back.

"Wasn't it?" agreed Kadija, "I simply breezed through the test. Didn't hesitate once on a spelling."

"Neither did I," said Dev, "It was as though each letter announced itself to me as I wrote them down."

Shannon nodded. "I could see them as well."

"I think that we all did, Shannon," Zach smiled, "It proves beyond any reasonable doubt that Elrond Hubbard's Grammarticus really works."

Chelsea-May smiled. "It truly is a magical book."

"Let's hope that the magic does not desert us before the week is out," warned Shannon.

But any fears they had were allayed the following day when they all sat the Grammar and Punctuation test. Even though they were in separate classrooms when taking the test, all six of them had exactly the same learning experience.

*'Insert a **comma** in the correct place in the sentence below'.* Zach silently read the first question, before continuing to read the sentence that followed.

'Although he was the youngest Tom was one of the tallest.'

Zach frowned for a moment, waiting for inspiration to strike. But he needn't have worried, for as soon as he read the sentence a second time, a twinkling comma appeared, hovering between the words *'youngest'* and *'Tom'*.

This is most excellent, Zach thought as he wrote the correctly punctuated sentence.

It was the same with the rest of the paper for Zach and his friends as they read through the remaining questions.

Correct sentences were identified and classified, punctuation added where needed with word classes underlined and labelled correctly.

The time easily passed without any of the children breaking into a sweat or worrying whether they had got the answers right or not.

They seemed to just know that they couldn't fail, that Grammarticus was still weaving its spell over them.

Wednesday's comprehension was much the same.

Sixty minutes that would normally have felt like sixty days passed with barely a hitch.

Zach and the others read, analysed and deciphered the texts given them, quickly answering the direct questions set.

Where inference was needed - no problem - all could give informed opinions and back up the reasons for their answers confidently, using examples from the text it related to in order to reinforce these points.

This feels so good, Zach thought as he took his seat for the unaided writing task that Miss Fletcher had added to their timetable that week. *One last test hurdle to overcome, a final week of school, then Easter holidays, here we come!* Zach smiled.

The confident look he had plastered all over his face wasn't lost on Miss Fletcher, who was still coming to terms with the incredible test results she was seeing from Zach, Shannon and Kadija.

"Last English task this week, my little kiddywinks," Miss Fletcher said, her patronising tones as shrill as ever, "I am pleased to see some of you have made real progress should early indications as to your scores prove to be correct when marked and moderated."

Zach smiled and looked across at Shannon and Kadija, who immediately looked away, causing Zach to turn back to face the front of the class – and stare directly into the milky-eyed gaze of Miss Fletcher.

"Indeed," she hissed, "Some of your scores are almost too good to be true, wouldn't you agree, Master Turner?"

Zach swallowed hard.

What did she know?

Was she onto him or was this just a bluff, seeing who would blink first?

He decided that he would lead with the *innocent* card first.

"Were it the case that one has achieved the results one has hoped for," Zach began, "Then it would be my just reward for all the hard work and effort that one has put in revising for these tests, which, in turn, would also endorse the wonderful support that we have had from your good self, Miss Fletcher."

Miss Fletcher sniffed. "Hard work and effort in revising…what, over a weekend, Master Turner?"

Zach could feel the sweat begin to form on his brow as the old teacher steered intently at him.

"I don't know how you've cheated, but this writing task will find you out, of that, I'm quite certain."

As Miss Fletcher turned to make her way back to the front of the class, Shannon worriedly looked up at Zach.

Does she know? Shannon mouthed.

How could she? Zach mouthed back as Miss Fletcher sat, perched on the end of her desk.

"Today, I want you to write a narrative story on a

subject of your choice. No input, no prompting, no guidance. Just write," Miss Fletcher looked at the clock, "You will have an hour today and an hour tomorrow to show me that you have what it takes to pass the Year 6 SATs tests, fairly and squarely."

"Fear not, dear lady," Zach said cheerily, "I will write a story of such style and structure that it will simply take your breath away."

"My dear Master Turner, I very much doubt that you will do no other than to prove that you've somehow cheated at your other tests," Miss Fletcher scoffed as she sat at her desk, "And if you do prove otherwise, then I will gladly eat my hat!"

Chapter 7

'*...and so the secret of Los Madres died with him that night,*' Zach smiled as he completed his story that Friday morning, '*The End.*'

He sat back and collected together the fourteen A4 lined sheets that he'd written his story on.

Fourteen double-sided pages completed in the time given to him and the rest on Year 6 since Miss Fletcher set them off the previous day.

Zach marvelled at the story, as though reading it for the first time.

Which, in truth, he was, given that he had no recollection as to what he was writing whilst he wrote it out.

It was just like a film that he'd once illegally watched around Antonio's house late one night, one of those cheaply made, badly shot B-movie horrors - Antonio always watched movies which were rated as 18, his parents not seeming to mind, or care greatly.

Zach recalled being so terrified that he hardly watched any of it, choosing to hide behind an extra-large, fluffy cushion instead.

But he still vividly remembered one scene where this psychic held a pencil and a paper and asked the spirit, who she claimed to be channelling, to write a message to the people who had asked to contact it.

The psychic's eyes then rolled into the back of her head as her hand began to write furiously across the paper before her, the text becoming more and more frenzied as she did so.

Zach had stopped watching and covered his ears once the psychic had started to scream after the pencil had worn away, her finger continuing to write the message sent from beyond the grave in her blood instead

That's what writing his story had been like.

Automatic.

Uncontrollable

Unstoppable.

As his eyes scanned through the perfectly written, neatly presented text, Zach looked for any obvious spelling mistakes, grammatical errors or missing words and incorrect punctuation.

There were none.

Zach marvelled as he read the adventure *he* had apparently written, the story and structure as good as anything he had ever read or had read to him.

There are fronted adverbials, subordinate clauses, Zach thought as he continued to read, *alliteration, similes, metaphors, personification, speech, consistent narrative voice use and it remains in the same tense throughout!*

It had everything he could ever have hoped for when writing a story.

In fact, it had everything that Miss Fletcher demanded when choking the children of their creativity when she lectured her class during their English lessons.

And more.

Much more.

Once Zach had read through *The Lost Treasure of Los Madres,* as he'd titled his story, he sat back and allowed himself the smuggest of smiles, lacing his fingers behind the back of his head, a gesture immediately witnessed and pounced upon by Miss Fletcher who glared at him.

"Have you finished, Master Turner?"

"Yes, Miss."

"You do realise that there is still half an hour to go until lunch."

"That I do, Miss."

"Oh. Have you read your story aloud, proof-read it and checked it for errors then?"

"Yes, Miss. Twice, Miss."

Miss Fletcher frowned. "And have you corrected your work?"

"No, Miss."

Miss Fletcher smiled like an alligator, ready to hungrily pounce on its helpless and unsuspecting prey. "Then I suggest that you do. After all, you need all the help that you can get, young man."

"No need to, thank you, Miss Fletcher," Zach grinned, "I'm more than happy with how my story has turned out."

"Don't say that I didn't warn you," Miss Fletcher scowled as she looked down at the textbook which was open on the desk before her.

When the bell rang for lunch, Zach joined the line of children waiting to hand their stories in to their teacher.

As they passed, he heard Miss Fletcher grunt as each story was placed on the desk beside her. It was only when he placed his on top of the growing stack of paper that the teacher looked up and fixed him with her piercing eyes.

"Thank you, Master Turner," she sneered, "I look forward with great interest to reading this."

"Thank you, Miss Fletcher," Zach smiled, "Make sure you're wearing your finest Easter bonnet when I see you Monday!"

Zach sat in his room that Friday night with slightly mixed feelings about his week.
He'd arrived home from school jubilant, Grammarticus had conjured up all that he and his friends had needed for their tests, a fact confirmed when they had all finally completed their lunchtime duties in the library.
Antonio and Dev had explained how simple the spellings had seemed to them, having failed every single spelling test they'd sat that year.
Kadija was ecstatic at finally being able to read properly, the letters not 'jumbling about on the page for once' as she took her comprehension test.
Chelsea-May smiled as she recalled her Grammar test, noting the same way the answers had magically appeared to her, which all of the friends agreed had happened to them too.
Even Shannon, normally the most guarded of individuals, was gushing about the way she'd written so fluently and easily during the unaided writing task, announcing to all who would listen that she had finally 'found her writing voice' and how she hoped to never have to relinquish the English skills she now had.
All of them also agreed that had Zach not been brave enough to have read from Grammaticus, then none of this would ever have been possible.
"Think nothing of it, my dear friends," he said happily, "Seeing you all so content and happy is ample reward for this humble youth."
The six of them then set about stacking the final,

repaired books onto the shelves, safe in the
knowledge that they were sure to pass their mock
SATs and avoid having to come in for extra lessons
over the course of the Easter holidays.

And that should have been that.

Except…

Except for a couple of strange and bizarre instances
that led to Zach being grounded for the weekend.

The first took place during PE that Friday afternoon.
Zach had partnered up with Shannon as they set off
on another set of gruelling exercise circuits laid out
by Mr Dickson, the inept coach the school employed
to cover PPA afternoons for their class teacher.

Whilst they were on the Star Jump station, Zach
spotting Shannon as she competed against Finlay
Jenner, Finlay's partner, Benny Benson, started to
make some rude remarks about the changes which
had recently, but naturally, started to happen to
Shannon's body.

"Don't be so rude," Zach had said, noticing how
flushed Shannon had started to become, "You're
embarrassing her."

"Me embarrassing her?" Benny sneered, "It's
embarrassing me watching her, mate!"

"Benny, stop it," Finlay panted, mouthing her
apologies on behalf of the obnoxious partner she'd
been forced to work with by Mr Dickson.

"Why should I?" Benny continued, "I was only
telling the truth, innit?"

"Put a sock in it!" Zach snapped, "Otherwise, I
will…"

The next few seconds were a bit of a blur for Zach.
Before he knew it, he was knelt over the prone figure

of Benny who lay startled beneath him, a long, red sports sock now protruding from his mouth, bulging from it like an over-sized crimson tongue.

"Get off him, Turner!" Mr Dickson bellowed as he ran towards the two boys, his arms moving faster than his short, stumpy legs as he did so.

Zach felt hands grasp his shoulders as Shannon and Finlay hauled him to his feet.

As he rose, he spotted Benny's naked right foot, his trainer lying about a metre away from him.

"What happened?" Zach, his mind just as bare as Benny's foot.

"You actually put a sock in it," Shannon grinned as the headteacher, Mrs Sandhu came marching over, having been sent for by the baffled cover teacher.

"Well, he did ask for it," Zach grinned.

But he wasn't grinning an hour later once his dad had been called to collect him from school...

"I'll have my pay docked for this," Zach's dad growled as the two of them walked up the small path that led to their terrace house, "You're lucky you didn't get suspended."

"A week of after-school detentions is punishment enough for the crime I committed," Zach replied, "I don't know what on Earth came over me."

His dad looked at him sympathetically as he searched for his front door key. "Did the kid Benny have it coming to him, son?"

"In a manner of speaking, yes," said Zach, adding, "He's always teasing Shannon about the way she looks."

"So you stuck up for your friend, right?"

Zach frowned. "Yes, I suppose so, though I have scant recollection of what I did."

"Looks like a little bit of jealousy got the better of you," Zach's dad said as he ruffled his son's head, "Like father, like son, eh?"

Zach wasn't quite sure what his father meant but thought it best to agree with him. "It would appear so, Father."

Zach's dad leant down and whispered in his son's ear. "If it were up to me, I'd let you off. After all, you were only defending the lady's honour, weren't you?" he said as he inserted the key into the lock, "However, I think your mum will take a much dimmer view of you fighting at school…"

Dad's words proved to be prophetic as, over dinner, Zach's mum began to preach to him how violence 'never solved anything' and that the strongest men 'use calm words carefully so that they don't have to use their fists to be heard.'

Zach sat, listened and was prepared to take the punishment meted out by his mum, which was 'no electronic devices for the entire weekend,' until his sister decided to add her two-pennies-worth.

"You're lucky Mum and Dad are so easy going," Emma began, "Rhiannon's brother got grounded for a week when he was caught fighting at school."

"Well it's a good job I'm not Rhiannon's brother then, isn't it?" Zach replied, already feeling irritated by his sister's interjection. He could tell that his sister was trying to wind him up, as usual, but was determined to keep his temper, knowing that he'd got off fairly lightly with the punishment he'd been given thus far.

However, Emma could sense his unease and, predictably, continued to subtly taunt her little brother. "You were also lucky to get away with the penalty the school gave you. If that had been Mr O'Dell, you'd have been suspended straight away."

"Well it wasn't and I'm not," Zach said, through gritted teeth, also aware that his mum had shot Emma a look, warning her to 'drop the subject'.

But his sister was warming to the task and beginning to hit her taunting stride. "You're lucky that Benny didn't just get up and wallop you. That's what will happen when you go up to secondary school."

"Emma…" Zach's dad warned as he sucked up another piece of spaghetti.

"I'm only looking out for him, Dad," Emma said sweetly, "That's all."

Peace eventually broke out around the Turner table for a few minutes, much to Zach's relief, as the four of them silently contemplated their preferred method of eating Mum's bolognese – twisting, chopping or noisily slurping the sauce-covered pasta.

"Zach's lucky that Benny's parents didn't get the police involved."

"Emma, that's enough," Zach's mum said firmly.

"Yes, Emma, please be quiet," Zach snapped."

"'*Emma, please be quiet,*'" Emma mockingly mimicked.

"Why don't you just stop talking rubbish," Zach snorted, "Your mouth is creating a terrible draught in here!"

Emma looked at him, for once, lost for words, before flicking her middle finger up at Zach. "Bite me…"

Apparently, Zach had been lucky that he hadn't broken Emma's skin, at least that's what his dad had shouted at him after finally prising his son's teeth off of his daughter's finger.

Now, little over an hour later, after the hysterics which had ensued around the dinner table, Zach sat on his bed, still struggling to come to terms with how and why he had suddenly transformed into a cannibalistic madman.

He desperately tried to recall any of the moments before his dad had jabbed him hard in the ribs, causing Zach to howl in pain, releasing his screaming sister's finger from his mouth.

Luckily for Emma, Zach's teeth were still a mixture of baby and adult teeth, but he'd still managed to give her a really nasty bitemark at the base of her middle finger.

His mum had quickly rushed the shocked teenager to the sink as Zach's dad grabbed his collar and frog-marched him to the foot of the stairs, ordering him up them and to 'not come down again until you are told to.'

Almost sixty minutes of torture and torment he'd now endured, first listening to the wails of his sister, then the torrent of anger that, first, his mother and, then, his father had launched at him, culminating in him being confined to his bedroom for the rest of the weekend.

When Zach apologetically asked as to what he would do about eating, he was told that he would eat alone in his room until he learned 'exactly what your mouth is supposed to be used for' by his despairing father.

As Zach's dad turned to leave the room, he paused

momentarily to look disappointedly at his son.
"I don't know what on Earth has gotten into you recently," he said shaking his head as he closed the door behind him.

Now, having had time to quietly reflect on the things that had happened to him that day, Zach was beginning to ask himself the very same question.

Chapter 8

"You actually bit your sister?" Shannon said incredulously as the two of them stood outside of Miss Fletcher's classroom.

"Indeed I did," Zach replied, "Though I am at a total loss as to why."

"So not only did you try to choke Benny on Friday," Shannon said, "You also tried to eat Emma too!"

Zach nodded as they watched Kadija arrive and wave to them from the back on the line.

He always felt better whenever he talked to Shannon about anything that was bothering him.

Zach was relieved to have a little normality after his weekend in isolation, plus, it was good to be able to talk to someone he openly trusted with what had happened.

This was especially true today after his mum had given him the cold shoulder that morning, much as she had for the previous two days.

His fate was further compounded by the fact that his mum had insisted she take him to school that day as she had 'lost all faith in him safely making his own way there after Friday's events.'

"I have been wracking my brains as to why I did what I did," Zach whispered as they saw Miss Fletcher march towards them, a little more flustered than usual.

"I have to admit it is all so very out of character for you, Zach," Shannon replied as Miss Fletcher fumbled with her keys before opening the classroom door, "Perhaps it was your way of letting off steam after all that testing last week."

"Perhaps," Zach replied as they entered the classroom, "But I can't help shaking the feeling that it's no coincidence I acted in such a manner after reading Grammarticus."

Zach and Shannon walked into the class as Miss Fletcher deposited the books she carried onto her desk before placing her coat on the vintage coat stand the eccentric teacher kept in the corner of her room.

As he watched her, Zach couldn't help but notice that there was something different about the usual routine Miss Fletcher religiously followed prior to every English lesson she took them for, but he couldn't quite place his finger on it.

"Is it me," Zach whispered, "Or is there something a little bit *off* about Fletcher today?"

"She's always off!" Shannon sniggered, continuing, "But, now you come to mention it, she does look a little greener around the gills today."

That's it, thought Zach as he looked at his unpleasant teacher who perched on the edge of her desk, like a vulture waiting to swoop down and feast on the body of its next lifeless victim.

But something still niggled him.

She still had a vampiric look to her, the teacher's skin looking as though it had never been touched by sunlight.

But, today, Miss Fletcher looked even more undead than usual, her skin having a clammy, pallid hue as she began to address the class.

She looks a bit mouldy today too, Zach thought as Mis Fletcher gestured for those still standing before her to take their seats.

"Good morning, *mes enfants,*" she sneered, her voice

as haughty as usual, despite her strange, sickly complexion, "I trust you all had a more relaxing weekend after the trials and tribulations of last week." Miss Fletcher's eyes fixed on Zach, seeming to somehow silently tell him that she knew what had happened on Friday, causing him to squirm in his seat slightly as she continued. "You'll be pleased to know that after a weekend spent marking and assessing your papers, the majority of you have made excellent progress and have a good chance of passing your SATs this year."

An almost audible sigh of relief echoed around the classroom as Miss Fletcher took her seat behind her desk. "Today, we will use this lesson for you to silently read to yourself, to a partner or to Mrs Kaur whilst I speak to each and every one of you about the results you achieved, as well as agreeing on the individual targets you will need to focus on over the next few weeks."

The noise levels in the class increased dramatically as chairs were scraped, bags dumped on tables and books produced whilst Mrs Kaur called for the first pupil to come and read with her as Miss Fletcher summoned her first, reluctant victim to her desk. "Wilde, to me. And don't forget your planner."

"Yes, Miss." Zach watched as a bespectacled boy he knew as Oscar walked gingerly to the front of the class.

One by one, a succession of children made their way to and from Miss Fletcher's desk, their faces betraying how much progress they had made during assessment week.

Or lack of progress, Zach thought as he observed the

look of dejection some of his classmates wore as they made their forlorn way back to their desks.

"Our turn soon," Shannon whispered as Miss Fletcher curtly shouted the next name on her class list.

But as the lesson went on, Zach noticed that although she was rapidly making her way through those who belonged to her English group, she had yet to summon either Zach, Shannon or Kadija, who sat happily reading to Mrs Kaur as the clock's hands fast approached lunchtime.

"Something's not right here," Zach whispered when the lunch bell rang, accompanied by the screeching sound of metal chair legs scraping the floor as thirty pairs of feet eagerly awaited their escape.

"Have a good afternoon, children," Miss Fletcher's voice said robotically, not sharing the sentiment that her words offered, "Shannon, Kadija and Master Turner, please remain at your desks. I'd like to talk to you collectively about your results."

Zach swallowed hard as he first looked at Shannon and then Kadija as the other members of their English set made their escape, the last one being told to close the door behind them as they left.

Miss Fletcher returned to her favoured position, sitting on the edge of her desk. Without uttering a single word, she cast her head back and forth, looking at each of the three terrified children in turn.

Unable to bear the uncomfortable silence any longer, Shannon raised her hand and began to speak. "Have we done anything wrong, Miss?"

Seeing her opportunity to also speak up, Kadija nodded. "Yes, Miss, have we all failed really badly in our mocks?"

Miss Fletcher tutted and shook her head slowly. "*Mais non, mon cher, au contraire!*" she mewed in French, a grin forming on her lips, making her look like an albino Cheshire cat, "You have all done exceptionally well. Too well, in my personal, and professional, opinion."

The three friends looked at one another, confusion now etched across their young faces.

"How can we do *too well*?" Shannon asked.

"Now, let me see," Miss Fletcher said, looking upwards, as though searching for the answers in the heavens. "You all scored 100% in your spelling, grammar and comprehension tests."

"Surely that's a good thing," Kadija replied, Zach nodding furiously in agreement.

"Oh, absolutely," Miss Fletcher said, "It's just that your results are *too* good. Perfect in fact. Too perfect."

Miss Fletcher reached behind her and grabbed some of the papers she'd kept there on the desk. "If I didn't know any better, I'd swear that you'd already seen the test papers and memorised the answers."

"But we didn't, Miss," Zach pleaded, "Honest, Miss."

"Honest, eh," Miss Fletcher sneered, "Hmmm…Then I thought to myself '*no, they couldn't have*' as only I knew which of the papers we would use and I only decided on those last Monday morning."

Zach let out a sigh of relief as Miss Fletcher scratched her chin, her fingers tracing a stray, wiry whisker before continuing. "Then I thought that you must have copied each other as your answers were the same," she looked down at the papers she held, flicking between them, "*Exactly* the same, right down to the very last word."

Zach could feel the fear rise up inside him as he watched Shannon make to protest, but Miss Fletcher raised a hand to instantly silence her. "But then I remembered that you all sat in totally different positions in the classroom, so that couldn't be the answer either."

"We didn't cheat, we promise," Kadija begged.

"Reluctantly, the fact is that I was inclined to believe you - except for the two darndest things," Miss Fletcher said, waving the papers she now held up in her hands, "Firstly, not only are your test papers all exactly the same in the way you have answered your questions, they also look like they've been written by the very same person!"

Zach squinted his eyes to look at the three comprehension sheets that Miss Fletcher waved at them.

She was right.

To the untrained eye, it did look like they had all been written by the same hand, the only difference being the names written at the top of each sheet and the choice of pen or pencil the writer had used.

Shannon looked at Chelsea-May and Zach before shrugging her shoulders. "I don't know what to say, Miss Fletcher, except that we all tried really hard to make sure we did our best for you."

"Hmmm," Miss Fletcher frowned, "I wish I could believe you, Shannon, I honestly do. And I admit that I have no real proof to back up my suspicions. Except..."

Here it comes, thought Zach nervously.

"Except for your unaided writing," Miss Fletcher

said, wiping her hand across her sweaty brow, "Which, I must confess, was some of the finest writing I have had produced for me by any pupil in nearly thirty years of teaching."

Zach beamed as he looked at Shannon and Kadija. "So, I made you eat your hat then!" he laughed.

"That you did, Master Turner, that you did…" Miss Fletcher nodded, "Though I do feel somewhat nauseous today after doing so. Remind me next time to choose something more palatable than my favourite beret. It appears to have greatly disagreed with me."

Zach sat, open-mouthed, as he looked at his teacher, trying to work out whether Miss Fletcher was joking or not.

Then, suddenly, he realised what it was about her morning routine that had seemed so different today. She'd only hung up her long, waterproof Mackintosh when arriving in class.

Normally, Miss Fletcher would make a big extravagant gesture and toss the small, round, flat-crowned woollen French hat she always wore onto the coat-stand before hanging her coat from it.

Every day, without fail.

Except for today.

Because, as Zach now realised to his horror, she didn't have her beret.

Because she had eaten it.

As promised.

Zach's story had been so good Miss Fletcher had actually eaten her hat!

Zach could feel a cold sweat wash over him, making him feel as clammy as Miss Fletcher looked as the old teacher continued, seemingly thinking it normal to have eaten an item of clothing she had so lovingly worn, year after year.

"Now, where was I? Ah, yes, your stories. Beautifully written. Engaging, humorous, exciting and adventurous, written with a maturity far beyond your years. I was, and am, truly astonished as to how three terrible writers such as yourselves could have produced such amazing pieces of work. However..."

Here it comes, Zach thought again.

"Whilst I admit that I am at a loss as to how you did it," Miss Fletcher sighed, "And can't prove that you did cheat, but, let's face it, *The Lost Treasure of Los Madres*, *The Last Treasure of Las Modres* and *The Lost Secret of Les Modresa* are a little too coincidental as titles, are they not?"

Zach, Shannon and Kadija sat wordlessly, not daring to utter a word for fear of incriminating themselves. After what seemed like an eternity, Miss Fletcher slammed both her hands on the desk beside her as she glared at the three shell-shocked pupils. "But, rest assured, children, from now on I will be keeping an eye on you three...a very close eye."

Zach, Shannon and Kadija screamed as one of Miss Fletcher's eyes suddenly popped out and stretched itself towards them, the optical nerve which normally attached it to her head extending out like a selfie stick as her eye surveyed each one of them in turn, before shooting back into its socket.

"Right, off to lunch with you then!"

Chapter 9

"What in heavens was that?" Kadija finally managed to ask after the three of them had sat in stunned silence, still in a state of shock in the dinner hall. "You did see that, didn't you?"

"It was hard not to," Zach replied as Antonio, Dev and Chelsea-May waved and made their way over to join them. "Her eyeball was literally millimetres away from mine!"

"Good morning?" Antonio asked as he placed his tray on the table and sat next to Zach.

"Not in so many words," Shannon replied as she began to retell the events of the strange day they'd all had up until that point.

"Fancy Francis pretty much said the same to us," Kadija finally said, "Though she kept her eyes firmly in her head as she did so."

"What about you, Dev?" Zach asked.

"My English teacher just praised me," Dev replied, "But then, there's none of you lot in the same set as me, so nothing would have looked out of the ordinary when my papers were marked."

"They're all bound to talk to one another soon though," Kadija said sadly, "Then we'll be for it."

Zach shook his head. "Noticing our work is the same is the least of our problems," he groaned, "There are bigger issues at play here."

"There is?" Antonio asked.

Zach, Shannon and Kadija stared at each other in total disbelief.

"Didn't you hear what we said?" Shannon said, "Miss Fletcher's eye randomly shot out of her head!"

"Oh that," Antonio replied, "I thought it was a hyperbole and that you were just exaggerating!"

"Me too," Chelsea-May replied, a horrid realisation of the truth now dawning on her, "That does seem a bit strange though."

"Seems a bit strange? It was horrific!" Kadija gasped.

"Did she look like one of those monsters off of Doctor Who?" Chelsea-May asked.

"Daleks," Zach replied sharply.

"No need to be rude," sniffed Chelsea-May, "I was only asking!"

"No, that's what they're called," Dev laughed, "Daleks."

"Yes, she did a bit," Shannon said, "But it was much more terrifying."

"I bet it was," Antonio said, "Any idea as to why it happened?"

Kadija shook her head, but Shannon shot Zach a glance. "Tell them about Friday, Zach?"

Five pairs of eyes immediately fell on Zach as he sighed and shared the chain of events that he had been involved in, first with Benny and then his sister Emma, sparing them all no gory detail, his friends' eyes growing wider with each sentence spoken.

"So is it you causing all of this?" Antonio eventually asked.

"It would appear so," Zach sighed, "I've been present each time something weird has happened. Ever since I read that damned book, I appear to be cursed."

"Not strictly true," frowned Dev, before adding, "But come to think of it, there was something slightly odd at the start of our English today. As we were waiting for our teacher after morning break, Archie Connor was hurrying to finish his crisps."

"What's so unusual about that?" Shannon asked.

"Lucy Li told him that he ate like a wild animal."

"So?"

"Well, before you knew it," Dev laughed, "Archie had tipped his crisps on the floor and was growling wildly whilst he ate them just as Miss came in. He got a right telling off."

Nervous laughed erupted around the table at the mental image Dev had created for them.

Except for Zach, who sat silently, a brief feeling of relief filling his body as Shannon turned to him and smiled.

"See, it's not just around you that these things are occurring."

"True," Zach replied, "It seems to be happening around all of us, probably because of the one thing that we all now have in common."

"Which is?"

"We were all stood together when I read those spells out of Grammarticus."

"But why would it cause such random and scary things to happen?" Chelsea-May asked.

Silence descended on the table again, save for the odd crunch of crisps as Antonio continued to eat his *Monster Munch*.

Suddenly, Shannon's eyes lit up. "Words. It's all to do with what was said just before each thing happened."

"You're right," Zach agreed, "The events that have happened exactly matched what was said just before them - *'Put a sock in it,' 'bite me,' 'keep an eye on you,'* and *'you eat like a wild animal!'*"

Shannon nodded. "Precisely. The book is making those types of sayings and sentences come true."

Dev frowned again. "So, if we say a simile or a metaphor, Grammarticus is making them come true?"

"It would seem so."

"But there are other types of things that have been said," Kadija said, "I can't for the life of me think what they're called though."

"Idiom," Zach replied.

"What's idiotic about that?"

"No, not idiot, *idioms*," Zach smiled, "Common phrases, proverbs or old sayings."

Kadija blushed, causing the others to laugh again, Zach included.

"If what you say is true," Antonio asked once peace had been restored after a disapproving glare from one of their lunchtime supervisors, "Then we've been extremely lucky so far."

"How do you mean?" said Chelsea-May.

"Well, what if you had told somebody to drop de-"

"Don't!" screamed Zach as he slapped his hand across Antonio's mouth, causing his friend's eyes to budge almost as much as Miss Fletcher's had, only to thankfully remain exactly where they were supposed to be.

"Zach's right," Shannon whispered, "We have to be really careful as to what we say and how we say it from now on. OK?"

Antonio nodded as Zach slowly lowered his hand, the impression of his fingers still evident on his friend's mouth. "I understand that we have to be careful when choosing what we say," Antonio said, adding, "But how do we control what others say around us?"

The six of them all looked at one another, for once at a total loss for words.

"We can't," Shannon replied, "Sooner or later, someone will say something around us and..." she clapped her hands to illustrate her point, fearing that the word she was about to say could actually cause an explosion.

"Shannon's right," Zach said, "There's only one way for us to sort this whole mess out?"

"And that would be..." Dev asked.

"By finding a spell in Grammarticus to reverse everything that it's done so far!

Chapter 10

As Zach stood outside the school gates early the following morning, he allowed his mind to wander back to the previous lunchtime.

Everyone agreed that reading again from Grammarticus was absolutely the right thing to do and that they should head straight to the library after school to get it over and done with.

When Zach reminded them that he had a week of afternoon detentions, Antonio had suggested they press ahead with it anyway, until Shannon reminded them that as Zach had been the one to have read from the book initially, then it should be he who reverses the spells. So they agreed to meet early the following day prior to their lessons and that they should avoid any opportunity to say or hear anything remotely suspicious in the meantime.

Fortunately, the curriculum for Monday afternoons in Year 6 consisted of French and Music, so there was little or no opportunity for anything out of the norm to be said.

However, home life had proven to be an entirely different matter for Zach though...

Grateful to still be given the cold shoulder by his parents – oh, the irony! – Zach had gone straight to his room and plugged his headphones into his iPhone to drown out any sound with the heaviest rock music he could find.

So effective was his self-exile that he didn't hear his dad come into the room, jumping with fright when his father gently touched his shoulder and mouthed the word 'dinner' at him.

Zach had nodded and followed him silently down the stairs.

Sat at the table, Zach had been forced to remove his headphones, which he reluctantly did, sitting quietly next to his dad as his mum plated up.

Noticing the empty seat where his sister normally sat, he asked his dad where Emma was, the shrugged reply and stern look Dad gave him told Zach everything he needed to know about his sister's unexplained absence.

Dinner was silently eaten, with the occasional question directed his way about school and what he'd learned that day, Zach confidentially answering, carefully measuring his response before doing so.

Everything was going swimmingly and without incident until midway through pudding – bananas and custard, Zach's favourite – when the front door slammed and Emma shot past the kitchen door and up the stairs to her room, shouting, "No dinner for me, I'm off to Shanice's house."

This instantly caused Zach's dad to leap from his chair.

"You come down here, right now, young lady," he shouted, "Your mum's already cooked and saved you some dinner."

"I never asked her to," came the snotty teenage reply, "I'm going out."

"You didn't say that you didn't want dinner," Zach's mum shouted from the table.

"Didn't know I had to give you a detailed description of all my movements," Emma shouted sarcastically. "Last time I looked it was a free country!"

"It'd be nice knowing what you're doing from one

minute to the next," Zach's dad replied angrily, "Especially as you've been treating this house just like a hotel recently…"

Zach shuddered almost as soon as the words had left his dad's lips, the kitchen suddenly transforming around him whilst Zach sat there, the table spinning rapidly, turning into a hotel's front desk, his mum's t-shirt and jeans transforming into a smart suit, a badge with the name *Maureen* pinned to her jacket.

Zach's chair glided to the side of what was now a hotel foyer as he looked at his dad, who stood in the doorway, dressed in a bellboy's outfit as his sister walked down the stairs, handing her key to him as she passed.

"Thank you, Turner," she said snootily, walking to the front door, her dad rushing to open it for her.

Emma handed him a pound coin as she strode through the door. "Keep the change," she smiled as Zach's dad tipped his hat toward her.

"You're most kind, madam."

Yes, Zach thought as his dad turned and whistled cheerily, *the sooner things get back to normal around here, the better for everyone!*

"Where are they?" Zach muttered, checking his watch again.

It was now 8.20 am and he knew that their window of opportunity in finding the spell they were looking for and performing it was rapidly running out.

Fortunately, as Zach tried to will the hands on his watch to magically slow down, he heard several footsteps approaching from behind him, accompanied by the sound of nervously excited chatter.

"You took your time, didn't you?" Zach huffed as Shannon and the others walked up to him.

"Sorry, our bus was late," Shannon explained as the six of them quickly began to walk across the playground toward the main entrance to the school building.

"That's all right," Zach replied nervously, "I was just a little worried we'd run out of time. We just need to hope that Mr Copthorne is about to let us in early again."

But as it turned out, there would be no such opportunity for them to sneak into the library.

Mr Copthorne was indeed there, but he was solemnly patrolling the two forbidding double doors, hazard tape stuck across both of them, a notice telling the reader to *'DO NOT ENTER'* attached to the tape.

"Morning kids," Mr Copthorne smiled, "I'm sorry, but you won't be able to go in there just yet."

Zach frowned. "But we only want to fetch a book or two for our lessons today. It won't take us long."

Mr Copthorne shook his head. "With the way things are in the library at the moment, nobody will be going in there today. We've apparently got an infestation."

"A what?" Antonio asked.

"An infestation," Mr Copthorne repeated, "The library is full of moths, hundreds of them! I'm waiting for the pest controller to come. I can't stand the blasted things myself!"

"What, pest controllers?"

"No…moths!"

The children looked at one another in bewilderment.

"Where did they come from?" Kadija asked.

"I've no idea," Mr Copthorne replied, "It was as clean

as a whistle when I locked the school last night. Then, this morning, hundreds of the blooming things with their papery wings were fluttering about everywhere! Makes me go weak at the knees just thinking about them!"

The site manager's body gave an involuntary shudder as Zach turned to look at the others.

"What do we do now?" Chelsea-May whispered.

Zach shrugged his shoulders. "Not a lot we can do at the moment, we'll just have to come back again tomorrow, I suppose."

Shannon turned back to Mr Copthorne. "Do you think it'll be sorted today?"

"I damned well hope so," Mr Copthorne replied, "Hate the idea of all of them bugs flapping around in there. Urgh!"

Despite their disappointment, the children couldn't help smiling at the thought of their burly site manager being so terrified of such a harmless little insect as a moth.

"Come on, we might as well hang out together for a bit before registration then," Kadija said as they waved goodbye to Mr Copthorne.

As they quietly made their way back through the corridor, Zach couldn't help shake the nagging feeling he had, something Antonio immediately spotted etched across his best friend's face.

"What is it?"

"What's what?" Zach replied as they all made their way back out onto the playground.

"That look."

"What look?"

"That look you always get when you're thinking,"

Antonio smiled, "I've told you before - thinking is a dangerous thing!"

Zach smiled briefly. "I was thinking about the moths. You don't think that they came from Grammarticus, do you?"

"Why would they?" Shannon said as the six of them sat on a low wall next to the school steps.

Zach shrugged. "Well, in the past few days, we've had book mites and bookworms, so why not book-moths?"

"But you didn't read the book yesterday," Dev replied, "In fact, none of us were anywhere near it."

"True, but what if these things appear every time something causes Grammarticus to work its magic, like when Miss Fletcher said she'd keep an eye on us?"

The friends fell silent for a moment before Chelsea-May piped up. "But Mr Copthorne said everything was OK with the library when he locked up last night."

Zach nodded but then frowned again. "True, but there were some weird things going on in my house last night with my sister and parents."

"What sort of things?" Shannon asked.

After recounting the events in the Turner household the previous night, before waiting for his friends to stop laughing hysterically, Zach repeated his earlier concerns. "So, what if it was Grammarticus that caused the moth infestation too?"

"Seems somewhat of a stretch," Chelsea-May replied, "Would there really be that many moths from just the one instance?"

"I agree," nodded Shannon, "Now I could understand

if there was more than the one thing happening at the same time, but I was really careful last night, as we all agreed." Shannon noticed the sheepish exchanges Kadija, Antonio and Dev gave with one another and frowned. "Right?"

"Well," Kadija began, "I may have inadvertently said something last night without actually realising it." Shannon looked fiercely at her friend. "Like what?"

"I was getting really annoyed with my brother," Kadija began, "He was in an awfully foul mood when he got in from college, ranting and raving at everyone and everything. He really ticked me off and we got into a blazing row and…"

"And?"

Kadija looked down at her shoes, seemingly finding something of real interest on the toe of one of them.

"Kadija!"

"I might have shouted at him…"

"And?"

"And sarcastically said that living with him was a real laugh-a-minute!"

Zach watched in stunned silence as Kadija then explained how her brother, Theo, had suddenly transformed into a clown, complete with a red nose and huge shoes, before then spending the entire evening in her parents' front room, delivering a comedy routine that had her whole house in stitches. "I didn't get to bed until after midnight! Theo just wouldn't shut up. I can still hear his flipping horn honking now!" Kadija looked at her friends anxiously, "Do you think that might have had something to do with the moths in the library?"

Zach nodded his head in frustration. "Oh, I think that

would go quite a long way to explaining why we have a sudden book-moth infestation! Anyone else have something that they'd now care to share with the rest of us?" Zach sighed and shook his head as he watched his best friend gingerly raise a hand.

"It was only a little thing," Antonio whispered, "And I only did it to help my mama as things have been a little tight since Papa lost his job and is now having to work nights at the superstore."

"What did you do?" Shannon sighed.

Antonio shook his head. "Nothing too dreadful, honestly. I knew Mama was struggling to cope with everything. So, after she got in from work last night, I hoovered, dusted and put the dinner on whilst she had a nap upstairs. She was really pleased and grateful. It really cheered her up."

"That's so lovely, but there's absolutely nothing wrong with that?" Shannon smiled as she wrapped an arm around Antonio's shoulders.

But Zach knew his friend far better than that. "What did you do?"

"Nothing," Antonio replied, "I didn't *say* anything."

"OK, so you didn't say anything," Zach repeated, "Then what did you *do*?"

Antonio sighed. "Mama was so pleased that she gave me this massive hug and said that I was so very special by doing what I did for her. So, I asked her how much I meant to her and Papa."

"And?"

Antonio grinned, sheepishly. "She told me I was worth my weight in gold! You should have seen it, Zachariah! Gold coins poured down from nowhere! It means that Papa can quit his stupid job. Now he and Mama won't ever need to worry about paying the bills again!"

"This just keeps getting better and better," Zach sighed, somehow sensing that there was yet worse to come, "What about you, Dev?"

"Pretty much the same I'm afraid, Zach," Dev admitted, "But I have to admit, I knew exactly what I was doing though. There I was, sat at home after having tea, thinking about all the things my friends have which my family and I don't…"

Suddenly, Antonio leapt up. "God, that's disgusting! Who's farted?"

His friends all looked at one another but when no one admitted it, Antonio sat done again. "Those that denied it, supplied it!" he muttered, holding his nose tightly.

"More like 'he who smelt it, dealt it'!" Zach laughed, quickly blocking his own nostrils with the sleeve of his shirt.

Once the foul stench has abated slightly, Shannon smiled gently at her friend again. "So, what did you do, Dev?"

Dev looked more crestfallen than before as his eyes began to well up. "I looked around our house, at my grandparents, my uncle and aunt, my parents, my brothers, my sisters and my little cousins and I got really angry, jealous and resentful, so…"

"So?"

"So I just said how amazing it would be if we were all stinking rich!"

Zach burst out laughing, despite himself. "Don't tell me - an avalanche of £5 notes just happened to rain down on you, I suppose?"

"£20 notes actually," Dev said glumly.

"Well, you could look a little happier, you're rich!" Kadija said.

"Yeah," Dev replied, "*Stinking* rich."

Shannon frowned at her friend before suddenly realising where the foul stench had come from earlier and the problem that Dev now undoubtedly had.

"You don't mean?"

Dev nodded sadly. "I'm afraid so. I've had six showers and eleven baths since last night, gone through four deodorants, three body sprays and a bottle of my grandma's perfume just to get myself ready for school. And as you can tell by the smell, it still isn't enough, I reek!"

Zach watched in horror as Dev raced off, a few flies following him as he sped towards the boys' changing rooms.

"Somebody had better cover for him at registration," Shannon said as the morning bell rang.

"Better than that," Zach replied, "We need to get our hands on Grammarticus, and soon, before Dev gases everyone to death!"

Chapter 11

That lunchtime brought no better news for the
children when returning to the library in the vain hope
that the emergency closure had been quickly resolved
and that it was again open for school business.
Instead, they found Mr Copthorne and Mrs Yellard
engaged in a fierce and extremely heated
conversation together.

A sign boldly declaring *'LIBRARY CLOSED UNTIL
FURTHER NOTICE'* was now hung across the
double-doors, a swarm of moths still active and
visible through the glass panels in each of them.

"And as I've already said," Mr Copthorne repeated,
the frustration painfully evident in his voice, "Every
time they thought that they'd cleared them out this
morning, another collection of moths seemed to
appear."

"But surely," Mrs Yellard insisted, "They must have
found the source of the infestation by now?"

Mr Copthorne sighed. "If they had, do you honestly
think that we'd be in this situation still?"

"We wouldn't have been 'in this situation' at all if
you had heeded my warning when installing the air
conditioning unit last summer."

"The air conditioning unit?" Mr Copthorne asked,
"What's that got to do with it?"

"Isn't it obvious?" Mrs Yellard sniffed, "That's where
the bugs must be coming from, there's nowhere else it
could possibly be!"

"Mrs Yellard, the moths aren't coming from the
aircon."

"How can you be certain?" Mrs Yellard huffed.

"Because."

"*Because,* what?"

"Because if the air conditioning unit had had the moths in them, then the whole of the school would have been infested by now."

"Hmmm," snorted Mrs Yellard derisively, turning to walk off, "And if I had wheels, then I'd be a bicycle!"

Zach, Shannon and the others didn't hang around long enough to see the obvious after-effects of Mrs Yellard's remarks, but the chime of a bell ringing and the rusty sound of an unoiled bicycle chain told then all they needed to know as they hurried their way along the corridor…

"This can't go on for much longer," Dev said, his eyes pale and his body aching all over, "I've almost rubbed myself raw just trying to keep myself smelling as fresh as I can. It's been five days already, surely we can go in there now?"

"Not according to Mr Copthorne," Shannon said that Friday lunchtime, "They are still no nearer to working out the source of the infestation."

"Isn't it obvious?" Zach groaned, "It's got to be Grammarticus."

"Probably," Shannon replied, "But only the six of us know that it could be the book."

"Somebody's going to have to do something soon," Kadija moaned, "If I hear another 'Knock, knock' or 'Doctor, doctor' joke from my brother, I'll think I'm going to go totally insane!"

Shannon frowned. "I feel for you, Kadija, I really do. This week's been intolerable. It doesn't matter how careful you are in minding what you say or how you say it, make even the slightest grammatical error or use the wrong choice of illustrative or figurative language and you are just asking for trouble."

It was true.

Although the six of them had been extremely careful in what they said, or who they said it to, since the library's sudden closure, they couldn't help being around people whose language was even more colourful than they'd ever realised before.

No wonder the moth infestation wasn't improving in the library. If anything, it was getting worse, and for good reason too.

Things had started to escalate after the children had gone to lessons on Tuesday, trying to mask their disappointment after their early arrival at George Orwell Primary that morning.

What used to be throwaway, casual remarks made in and around Zach, Shannon and Kadija before, during and after their lessons, now seemed to carry a hidden threat, with a more ominous tone as the three friends watched and waited for the repercussions of each phrase, or saying, innocently spoken by friends, family, peers and adults alike

For example, whilst crossing the playground, they heard Benny Benson sneer, 'What's the matter, you chicken?' as he goaded another helpless victim during morning break.

Admittedly though, they couldn't contain their laughter as the bully was cut down to size after he was chased remorselessly around the playground by the Year 4 that'd he'd dared, the tiny girl flapping her arms as she clucked and squawked after him, nipping and pecking his bottom viciously.

Then, after break, in English, Zach, Shannon and Kadija kept a low profile as Miss Fletcher watched the three of them intently, her eye rolling around uncontrollably in her head whilst they all completed their writing activities.

As the class was dismissed and the three of them scurried out past her, they ignored Miss Fletcher's shouted remark that it was no use 'ignoring the elephant in the room.'

Zach, Shannon and Chelsea-May ran even faster when they heard a large trumpeting sound echoing behind them and Miss Fletcher calmly say, 'There, there, Nellie dear, mommy's here!'

Strangely though, when Shannon snuck back into class some ten minutes later to retrieve her school bag, there was no sign of either the mad-teacher or the strange pachyderm, except for a large pile of steaming elephant dung in the middle of the classroom.

Over the course of the week, not one of the friends fared much better than the others, being the cause of, or party to, other shenanigans caused by magic and mischief unleashed by Grammarticus.

Kadija had been the first to have a narrow escape on her way to school one morning. She lived the furthest away, the bus picking her up first on the school run it undertook through St Godrics and the surrounding villages every day before and after school.

However, before even catching the bus, Kadija had to first set off on a fifteen-minute walk from the housing association home she lived in on the very outskirts of the town just to reach the bus stop itself.

By rights, she shouldn't have even been going to the

same school as her friends still, her family being forced into moving house after numerous run-ins with their neighbours for the two years previously. But her family, being the idle layabouts that they were, failed to inform the school of their change of address, so fortunately for Kadija, she was still able to continue to attend George Orwell Primary School.

However, that morning, just as she was leaving, her elder brother had laughed at her, saying that she was going to get soaked as it was 'raining cats and dogs' outside.

Kadija had taken her life in her own hands as she ran along the streets, dodging a downpour of Pugs, Pekinese and Persian dogs and cats respectively, the animals landing on the pavement beside her, before, nonchalantly, wandering off.

The sounds of caterwauling and howling echoed around her as bodies thumped against the roof of the school bus, paws pounding and claws scratching as the driver whistled his way through the early morning traffic.

"Thankfully, it looks like it's going to blow over soon," the bus driver shouted as a torrent of Chihuahuas and Bichon Frise bounced off the windscreen, looking none the worse for wear as they rolled into the gutter next to some confused looking Siamese and Sphynx kittens.

Luckily, the sky had cleared long before reaching school, but her friends looked horrified as Kadija retold the near catastrophe – or should that have been *dog-and-catastrophe* – that had almost befallen her that morning.

"Look on the bright side," Antonio had said, trying to

console his friend, "It could have been worse."
"How can anything be worse than being pelted by pets?" Kadija asked.
"Your brother could have told you that it was pis-"
"Antonio, don't!" Shannon scolded.
"Persistently raining," Antonio laughed, quickly correcting himself, averting the terrible possibility of a sudden downpour of yellow rain showering the school...

Meanwhile, Dev, having regularly sprayed himself with some cinnamon-scented air freshener he'd found after sneaking into Mr Copthorne's unlocked and unguarded office earlier in the week, had tried to avoid as much contact as he could with his fellow students outside of lessons.
However, he couldn't help but bump into Benny Benson and his band of bully brothers on the way home from school early one evening
Benny, who was as poor at learning from his mistakes as much as he was at learning anything else, and his dense cronies were hanging around the swings in the park which ran adjacent to their school.
Dev felt his heart sink as he walked towards the four boys, each of them sporting the same buzz-cut hairstyles, turned-up trouser hems and rolled up polo-neck shirt sleeves that were their gang's signature look.
"Hey, boys," Benny shouted as Dev tried to pass without acknowledging them, "Can you smell... *something*?"
Joshua Ashpole, an equally obnoxious boy, sniffed the air. "Smells like curry."

"Nah," sneered Benny, "Even that foreign muck don't smell that bad!"

"It must be Panesar then!" Joshua spat as the four boys laughed, holding their noses with one hand, whilst waving their other hand underneath their nostrils.

Dev stopped and sighed deeply.

Normally he would let school teasing wash over him, ignoring it, letting the insult pass him by.

But he'd been taught from a very early age that where matters concerned the colour of his skin, or his culture and beliefs, that he should not turn a blind eye and accept any form of prejudice or racism.

So Dev turned and squared up to the four boys.

He knew that he was at a disadvantage, numerically – four against one – and physically, each of Benny's gang being considerably larger than he.

But if there was one thing Dev was not, it was a coward.

"Gentlemen," he said politely, "It is rude and impolite to address me so. I am as British as you whilst still very proud of my Indian heritage."

"*Gor blimey guvnor!*" Benny mocked in a thickly accented parody of Dev's voice, "Doesn't our little brown friend talk all funny like?"

"Yeah, go home," Joshua Ashpole shouted, "Your kind aren't welcome here. This is our country!"

"*Your* country? *My* kind? The British government welcomed my ancestors here after the Second World War," Dev said defiantly, "I've as much right to live in England as you fascists do!"

"Yet you still don't know how to talk proper, do you?" Benny shouted, looking at his friends for their idiotic approval, which they predictably gave, "Go on, push off, go deliver a takeaway somewhere!"

Dev breathed deeply, trying to suppress the anger he felt rising from deep within him. Then he smiled as a mischievous idea soon came to mind.

Don't do it, you're better than that, his conscience said, but it was too late, Dev had made up his mind as to his response, no matter the consequences.

"At least I don't talk out of my backside, like you and your friends do…"

Instantly, Benny and his gang's mouths sealed over, with no visible trace that a natural opening in their faces ever existed.

Then…

Thpptphtphphhph…

Phhhtttttttt…

Thrpppppppppppp…

Fffffffffffffff…

Dev stood and watched the chaos unfold momentarily before he turned and walked off, suitably satisfied he'd had the last laugh.

The cacophony of loud, crude, rude toilet sounds and disgusting farting noises that Benny's gang's bottoms made as they tried to swear, shout and hurl insults and protestations at Dev showed no sign of abating long after the slight Anglo-Indian boy who'd bested them in their verbal battle of wits had disappeared into the distance…

Chapter 12

Whilst each and every one of them witnessed, or had caused, something weird and wonderful to happen that week, it was poor Antonio who ended up suffering the worst after-effects of the magic and madness that was being unleashed on St Godrics by Grammarticus.

Despite a couple of - dare I say it - *slip-of-the-tongue* moments, Antonio had managed to keep himself from causing any further mischief and mayhem to happen for almost the entire week.

Almost.

In truth, when it happened, it wasn't even Antonio's fault, it was just his back luck to be in the wrong place at exactly the wrong time.

A lavish party had been thrown at the local pizzeria on Thursday night to celebrate his grandmother's seventy-fifth birthday.

Even though it was a school night, Antonio, the youngest grandchild was expected to attend. He was Nonna's favourite, the only male grandchild that her five children had produced, in England or back home in Italy.

All Nonna's children and grandchildren who lived in and around St Godrics had gathered together, as expected, to celebrate the milestone age she had just reached.

What Nonna didn't expect though was Enzo, her oldest son who she had not seen in almost ten years after a heated row about the woman he had finally decided to end his bachelor days for, was her surprise birthday gift, having secretly flown in from Tuscany just for the occasion.

The look on Nonna's face as he walked in, holding his newborn baby girl, brought a tear to everyone's eye that night, including Antonio's.

An evening of food, wine, music and laughter ought to have ended perfectly and without incident.

And it almost did, were it not for an innocent remark made by Francesca, Enzo's much younger wife.

As she sat at the table happily talking to Antonio's mother and father, Antonio ran back from the dancefloor to grab a drink of coke, refuelling himself, ready to dance the rest of the night away with his many, female cousins.

"And this, Francesca," Antonio's mother said proudly, "is our son, Antonio Junior."

"Si, Si," Francesca said happily, "I can tell, he is *bella,* eh, I mean, he is handsome."

"Thank you," blushed Antonio, "They say I take after my father when he was a young boy."

"No, little Antonio," a loud voice boomed as Enzo lifted him up in a great, big bear hug, "You are not as ugly as he was, or is still!"

Nonna smiled and laughed as uncle and nephew were reunited after so many years apart.

Wishing to please his mother further, Enzo decided to pay her the ultimate compliment.

Unfortunately, it proved to be at Antonio's expense.

"No, my little man, you have definitely inherited the good looks which flow down the female side of our family," Enzo said, winking at Antonio, "In fact, I'd go as far as to say that you are the spitting image of your dear Nonna..."

The sight of the little old woman, with wiry grey hair

and a bottom almost as wide as the pathway she walked on shocked Zach and Shannon as she shuffled into the playground the following morning.

They were even more surprised when the old lady, dressed head to toe in black, a shawl flung over her shoulders, walked straight up to them and stared squarely into their eyes.

"This isn't even remotely funny anymore," the old woman said angrily as she approached them.

Zach was so transfixed by the hairy mole which bobbed up and down on her top lip that, at first, he didn't notice that the woman spoke in a strangely familiar voice.

"Antonio?" Shannon asked, prodding her friend in the chest, to see if it was real or just very heavily padded. But it wasn't padding - they were definitely real!

"Keep your hands to yourself!" Antonio shouted, slapping Shannon's hand away, "You've got to help me. Grammarticus has somehow turned me into an exact copy of my grandmother!"

"I suppose we'd better call you *Nonnantonio* now then! *Nonnantonio*? Get it?!" Zach laughed loudly, struggling to contain his amusement.

Antonio fixed him with a steely look. "It's a good job that I'm a lady, otherwise I'd tell you exactly what I'm thinking at this precise moment! How on Earth am I supposed to come to school looking like I'm over sixty years too old for it?"

"What do your family think?" Shannon asked, biting hard against the inside of her lip to stifle her urge to laugh hysterically.

"Nothing," Antonio sighed, "It's as though I've looked like this my entire life! No one's noticed anything different about me. All of them seem to think I've always looked like this, even Nonna herself!"

And that was the strangest thing of all.

No matter what happened around any of the children that week, no one else seemed to care, notice, comment or even remark on the strange events and peculiar occurrences being caused by Grammarticus. It seemed to be that only the six of them realised that there was something very different happening.

Only they appeared to notice the world changing around them, one word, sentence or phrase at a time. People only seemed to sit up and take notice when something painful or dangerous happened following an off-the-cuff remark or thruway comment, which, thankfully, had proved to be a rarity.

However, one disastrous incident eventually occurred and when it did, it was incredibly painful, upsetting and traumatic for those involved.

It was very much a case of saving the best for last at the end of such a strange, school week.

Or should that be the worst for last, as witnessed by Zach and his friends that Friday?

(Whisper it quietly but the events they watched unfold before them proved to be the final straw, the one which ultimately broke the camels' back for our hapless heroes!)

The whole of Upper Key Stage 2 had been summoned and were gathered in the hall to watch a specially commissioned play featuring members of Miss Francis' amateur dramatic company, *Adhoc Havoc*. Keen to pinch a penny or two, she had arranged for her friends to perform a play highlighting the dangers of social media misuse to the children.

Having excitedly introduced the production, Miss Francis hurriedly rushed backstage and could audibly be heard to wish her fellow performers good luck in the time-honoured and traditional manner that actors use time and time again.

"Break a leg, everyone!" Miss Francis cheered behind the curtain, causing Zach to bite his lip whilst Shannon shook her head in alarm and dismay.

"Oooh, famous last words, methinks!" Chelsea-May sighed in resignation as to what was almost certainly about to happen next...

It was difficult to tell whose screams were louder, those of the six cast members, whose legs snapped instantaneously, the crunching of bones echoing around the school hall.

Or the screams of the children in the audience as they watched on in horror as Miss Francis and her fellow thespians crawled across the stage, begging for help from the panic-stricken adults who'd hoped for a quiet hour or so of non-teaching time.

Either way, by the time the last ambulance had transported its incapacitated passengers to the closest accident and emergency department, Zach and his friends knew they couldn't wait any longer without attempting to break the spell Grammarticus had them all under.

"But how can we undo all of this is we can't even get our hands on the damned book?" Kadija asked, having met with her friends at the school gates while they awaited Zach's release from his final detention that week.

"Search me," Antonio said, soon realising his error as four pairs of hands frisked his body and foraged around in his clothes, causing him to laugh hysterically as Zach finally approached.

"Zach, help," Antonio cried, "I can't take this any longer."

"Neither can I," agreed Zach, "I walked past the library on my way here. There's still no chance of getting hold of that infernal book."

"Then, we have to accept that life is going to get a whole lot stranger then," sighed Kadija.

"Not necessarily," Zach replied, "The one good thing about detention is the fact that you have time to reflect and think about life, amongst other things."

Shannon looked at the others. "And did you come up with a way to help us out of the sorry predicament that we currently find ourselves in?"

"Indeed I have, my dear friend," Zach grinned mischievously as he began to walk off whilst the others still stood and stared at him.

"Not cool, Zach, that's such bad form!" Dev shouted after his friend, "Tell us what you've got planned!"

"Yeah, Zach," Antonio said, chasing after him, "What other way is there to solve this blasted conundrum?"

"It's quite simple," Zach beamed, "If we can't get hold of the book itself, then we need to go to Plan B."

"Which is?"

"If we can't lay our hands on Grammarticus itself, then we'll do the next best thing," Zach smiled, "We'll have to go find its author, Elrond Hubbard, instead!"

Chapter 13

Shannon's house had been chosen as the base of their covert operations the following morning. Partly because it was the one most central for all six friends to get to from their homes.

But mainly because of the fact that she would be home alone, as Shannon was most weekends, her parents having to work long shifts, both days.

This suited the children well as it meant that they wouldn't be disturbed during their quest for Elrond Hubbard.

Each one of them had arrived armed with a mobile device as a result of the message that Zach had texted them that morning.

"Why do we all need one?" Chelsea-May asked as they gathered around Shannon's kitchen table where Shannon now sat, iPad in hand.

"Because last night," Zach began, deliberately selecting the chair nearest to Shannon, "When I again asked my father if he knew where Mr Hubbard was now, he just shrugged his shoulders."

"Still doesn't explain what we need our mobiles for," huffed Antonio, who had appeared to have adopted his grandmother's grumpiness and impatience, as well as her elderly looks."

"I was just getting to that."

"Well, you'd better hurry," Dev said, sniffing his armpits, "I reckon I've about ten minutes before I'll have to use Shannon's bathroom to freshen up. My pits and bits are getting awfully sweaty and will stink the house out pretty soon!"

"Too much information!" Kadija gasped, covering

her eyes, "But now you've said it, my mind can't unsee it!"

Zach smiled. "It was my sister who gave me the idea, actually. As mum served her breakfast and dad cleaned her room, Emma said if I was that desperate to know where he was, I could always have a look in the phone book to see if he still lives nearby."

"No more books," Antonio snapped, "This one has been more trouble than its worth."

Shannon patted Antonio's knee. "There, there dear," she teased, "Why don't you have a nice cup of tea and a lie-down."

Antonio raised his middle finger right in front of Shannon's face.

"What an example to set your grandchildren, Nonnantonio!" Zach laughed, causing the others to burst out into hysterics.

"I've two words for you," barked Antonio, "And the second one is *off*!"

"Charming, I'm sure," Dev smiled as Shannon started to tap the screen on her tablet. "When we said *phonebook*, I meant the online version of course." Antonio allowed his temper to cool as Shannon negotiated the telephone book homepage.

"Basically," Zach said, "We just type his name into the search bar and hit ENTER. The website will find the closest matches. Then, using our phones, we'll take it in turns to phone the numbers we find there."

"Sounds like a plan," Antonio grinned as Shannon typed *HUBBARD* into the *name* search field, followed by *CAMBS* in the county search.

"Why *CAMBS*?" Kadija asked as a succession of names scrolled down the screen in front of them.

"If he was still in St Godrics itself," Shannon said as she peered at the screen, "Then surely he would have been seen out and about the town by our parents after he was forced out of the school."

"And as there have been no sightings of him at all," Zach added, "It's safe to assume that he doesn't live in St Godrics."

"But as we live in such a large county," Shannon continued, "There's a fair chance that he or his family live somewhere nearby instead."

"That's if he's still alive, of course," Zach said ominously.

Shannon nodded grimly and began to scroll down the list of names that had filled the webpage.

"Thirty-seven listings, wow!" Dev said, "That'll take ages."

"True," Shannon said, typing her tablet screen furiously," But let's look at those in a five-mile radius first."

"How are you going to do that?"

"Simple. I'll filter the search to those initials which include an *E* and are closest to the centre of St Godrics by their postcode and try those first."

Thirty-seven names had now been whittled down to nineteen *Hubbards,* all listed alphabetically on the screen before her. "There, that's much better."

"That's still a fair few to get through," Chelsea-May moaned.

"Three phone calls each," Zach said, adding, "Shannon and I will call the additional number at the end of our search."

Zach began to scribble numbers down on post-it notes and handed them out as each of the friends pulled their mobile phones from their pockets.

The next few minutes were spent, waiting for calls to be answered, messages being left on answerphones and questions asked that were either politely, or abruptly, rebuked, as each of the six searched for their man;

"Hello, is that Mr Hubbard? Oh, sorry madam…"

"No, miss, I promise you, I'm not going to ask you if you've had an accident in the past five years…"

"My name is Dev Panesar and my number is…"

"Yes, my mum lets me use the phone on my own…"

"No this isn't Brian…"

"Yes, I can use a potty too, dear, now please could you put your mummy or daddy on the phone…"

"And a very good day to you…charming!"

As each unsuccessful call ended, another name was struck off the list, leaving only two Hubbards finally left to call.

"It's no good," Dev sighed, shaking the second of the two bottles of body-spray he'd already used that morning. He threw the empty can to the floor and began to ring the second-to-last number, closely watched by his friends, "This is going to be a total waste of time and eff-"

"Hello?" a woman's voice suddenly interrupted from the other end of the line.

"Oh, I'm sorry," Dev half-yawned, "I was looking for Mr Elrond Hubbard. I'm so sorry to have disturb-"

"What do you want him for?" the woman asked impatiently.

Dev swallowed hard, as he mouthed, *I think I've found him to his friends*. "Well, er, we need his help regarding a book he wrote."

A pause on the other end of the call caused Dev to half-expect the phone to be cut off and the line go dead. Then he heard the one word that they'd all been desperately hoping to hear.

"Grammarticus?"

"Yes, yes, that's the one!" Dev said excitedly, nodding at his friends as he held a free thumb up. Zach raced across the room to join his friend, pressing his ear next to Dev's head, holding his nose as he did so. "We could really use his help and advice."

"What do you know of the book?" the woman asked, the suspicion she obviously felt now rising in her voice.

"Well, we've been using it as a textbook in school and we would like to ask Mr Hubbard is he would, er...talk about it and if, er...he would, er..." Dev stuttered, "autograph it for us?"

"Autograph it?" Kadija whispered at Dev, who shrugged his shoulders in response.

Another pause. "You have a copy of my father's book?"

"Yes. Yes, we do."

Another pause, longer this time. "How do I know you actually do have a copy of Grammarticus and that this is not one of those *prank* calls?"

Dev looked desperately at Zach for help.

Zach took the phone from him. "*'English is the most beautiful, but difficult language in the world to master,'*" he said, reciting the very first lines he'd read from the book almost perfectly from memory, "*'an almost uncontrollable beast...'*"

He thought that he heard the woman almost sob on the other end of the line before she breathlessly replied. "That sounds just like my father's words. We live at The Old Rectory in Buckle End. Do you know where that is?"

Zach nodded, recognising the name of the quiet parish which lay on the outskirts of the town, before remembering to answer. "Yes, I do."

"Good. Come this afternoon," the woman said humourlessly before adding, "But, be warned – you'd better be telling me the truth, or you'll come to regret it."

Chapter 14

Three hours, two bus journeys, one tea-stop and four loo-breaks later - Antonio hated his now seventy-five-year-old bladder! - the six friends found themselves making their way up a quiet, pot-holed lane that led to the Old Rectory, which had now been converted into the home of Elrond Hubbard and his daughter, Nancy. Zach could feel his stomach tighten with every step he took towards the former church building. He looked across at Shannon, who walked beside him.

If she feels as nervous as I do, he thought, *then she's damned better at hiding it.*

"So, what's the play when we get there?" Dev called as he followed behind with the others, applying yet more deodorant to his red-raw armpits, the shirt's material sodden around them.

"I'm not sure, yet," Zach confessed as the Old Rectory loomed before them, "Thought that we'd let Hubbard's daughter do all the talking first and then we'd fill in the blanks after."

"Well, let's hope she's a little friendlier than how she sounded on the phone."

"Come on, Dev," Kadija said as they opened the gate which led into the Hubbards' neatly kept front garden, "You heard what she said about hoax callers. I'd be pretty suspicious too if anyone I didn't know called me up, right out of the blue."

"Kadge's right," Shannon said as their pace slowed the closer they got to the imposing oak door at the front of the property, "And if what we've been told is true, they've more reason than most to be wary of any strangers asking anything about Grammarticus."

Shannon stood and looked pensively at the door, before turning to Zach. "Ready?"

"As ready as I'll ever be," Zach replied, adding, "Though it should be Dev and I that she sees first after speaking to the two of us on the phone."

Shannon nodded and stepped back as Dev sprayed himself with some floral body spray for the umpteenth time that day, before he pulled himself up to his full height as he loudly knocked on the door.

The children stood anxiously, with bated breath, as they waited for the door to be answered.

"You don't suppose that they've gone out," Dev whispered, making to lift the door knocker a second time, just as the door suddenly swung open.

"Good afternoon, Nancy Hubbard," a tall, pleasant looking woman said, extending her hand toward Zach as she looked down at the two boys. She lifted her head and frowned at the others stood behind them. "I didn't expect there to be so many of you. Nor did I expect you to bring your granny either."

Antonio bristled and went to speak, but Kadija wrapped a calming arm around him.

"Apologies, Miss Hubbard," Dev said, "But when our friends found out that we were going to meet the famous Elrond Hubbard, they insisted on coming with us. We're all such huge fans of his work!"

"Plus, we couldn't leave my poor nan, home alone," Zach smiled, "She might wee on the sofa again."

Nancy eyed the six of them with suspicious eyes which suddenly softened as she smiled warmly.

"Quite," she said softly before sending a hand out before her. "Now if I can have the book please."

Zach shot Dev a worried look. This was something

that he hadn't planned for in every scenario he'd previously played out in his head on the long journey here.

"I would rather give it to Mr Hubbard so that he could sign it, in person, himself," Zach lied, "I'd love to meet and speak with him to discuss how he came to write the book."

"There's not much chance of that I'm afraid," said Nancy sternly, "He's not spoken to anyone in almost thirty years." Nancy clicked her fingers, "Now, please just hand me the book."

"Well, you see, Miss Hubbard," Zach said, "We don't *actually* have the book with us."

"But we know where it is," Dev added.

Nancy paused and looked at the children as though carefully considering her response or the next course of action. "Sorry, no book, no meeting. Goodbye."

Zach and Dev looked at each other in desperation as Nancy began to close the door.

"Please, Miss Hubbard," Zach shouted, "We really do need your father's help. There is something really odd about the book that we don't understand and can't control."

"It's not our problem," Nancy said as she continued to shut the door.

"YES... IT...IS..." a metallic sounding voice echoed in the hallway behind her, "PLEASE...LET...THE... CHILDEN...IN...NANCY...LET'S...HEAR.... WHAT...THEY...HAVE...TO...SAY...FOR... THEMSELVES..."

Zach and Dev tried to stand on tiptoe to peer behind Nancy to where the voice had come from.

But all they saw was the brief sight of what appeared

to be a motorised vehicle disappearing into a room at the end of the hall.

"Well," Nancy sighed, "I suppose you'd all better come in."

Zach waved at the others to join him and Dev as they stepped over the threshold past Nancy Hubbard, who had moved to one side of the door for them.

"Turn left into the living room," she said, sniffing the air repeatedly, before raising a hand in front of Kadija and Antonio, "You two wait here. I'll go and see if I've any plastic sheeting for you, dear…"

It took less than half an hour for Zach and the others to explain to Nancy about Grammarticus, how they'd come across it and what they knew about it. They stuck to the story that the children had agreed, leaving out everything magical that had happened for fear of initially scaring the Hubbards off from helping them.

"So you see," Shannon concluded, "We were hoping that your father would be able to tell us more about Grammarticus and how we may be able to use it more effectively in our learning."

"My father is an old man," Nancy said sadly, "And most troubled and unwell. Some days are better than others, today not being one of them, unfortunately."

"Please, could you just ask him?"

Nancy shook her head before taking a sip from her tea. "And even if I were to ask, what makes you think he could, or would help you?"

"Because," Zach replied, "he might see it as a way of restoring his reputation after what he supposedly did before."

Nancy bit her lip and frowned as though struggling to control her patience and temper. "*After what he* *supposedly did…*just what do you mean by that?"

Zach swallowed hard, looking at Shannon and the others for their reassurance. "You know, how he helped his students to cheat and pass their tests."

Nancy Hubbard visibly bristled at Zach's suggestion. "I think you have been seriously misinformed about my father, young man," she said through tightly gritted teeth, "It's high time someone else knew the real truth about my father and that damned book…"

If explaining their fictitious reasons for being there had taken the children little to no time at all, hearing Nancy recount the whole sorry story of Grammarticus and her father's part in its history took much longer. Considerably longer.

Nancy explained how her father had been a very successful headteacher and Literacy consultant in London before taking early retirement, moving to St Godrics with her mother, who had been born and raised in the town before meeting her future husband.

"They'd only lived here for a little over three months when my mother died unexpectedly."

"I'm so sorry," Chelsea-May said, tears welling up in her eyes.

Nancy smiled. "It's all right, thank you. It feels like a lifetime ago now, to be totally honest with you."

She continued to tell the children how her father was then left all alone, in a town and community where he hardly knew anyone.

"At least he had you," Antonio said sympathetically.

"That's kind of you to say, dear," Nancy smiled, patting his wrinkled-stockinged leg, "Unfortunately I was already in my second year at university in Newcastle when Mum passed. I offered to quit my degree straight after the funeral, but Dad was having absolutely none of it."

"So what did your father do?" Zach asked.

"Just what he'd always done before," said Nancy, "He threw himself back into the two greatest loves of his life - other than my mother that is – his books and the history of the English language."

Nancy explained how to further fill his time, her father had joined *The Tome Raiders Club*, a group dedicated to searching for rare, legendary and unusual books, supposedly lost to time and history.

"My father was obsessed with finding the lost works of Roger Bacon which he believed would help him finally unravel Bacon's legendary *Cipher Code* that he'd come so close to solving on several occasions previously."

"And did he?" Shannon asked.

"Not initially," Nancy said, shaking her head, "He thought that he'd cracked it once or twice before but, each time there was always a vital piece of the puzzle missing. However, through *The Tome Raiders*, he met a man who changed his and ultimately, my life forever."

The children listened intently as Nancy retold how Hubbard had become friendly with a fellow *Tome Raider* and how, over a pint of warm ale one night, they'd discovered a mutual love of books of a mystical and mysterious origin and nature, sharing an interest in unravelling the secret of Bacon's long-lost, Cipher Code.

"My father was then invited to join the local research lodge that his new friend was already a member of," sighed Nancy.

Shannon looked at her friends, who seemed as clueless as she was. "I'm sorry, Miss Hubbard-"

"Nancy," Nancy corrected.

"Sorry, Nancy," Shannon repeated, still feeling uncomfortable when calling her by her first name, "But what is a 'research lodge'?"

"Now it's my turn to apologise," Nancy smiled, "It is a branch of the Freemasons, who are an exclusive and secretive society. There are different types of lodges, but a research lodge is devoted to Masonic research."

Zach knew that they all were none the wiser, judging by the puzzled looks on his friends' faces, but no one dared admit it, least of all he.

If they were a secret society, then they can't have been up to any good, he thought as Nancy continued.

"It was there that he met with other like-minded individuals. Men of high social standing and intellect, who held power and influence in the local area. Businessmen, councillors, members of the nobility etc. It was here he met the governors of various schools in and around St Godrics."

Nancy explained how, over the course of a number of lodge evenings and meetings, her father had come to think of these people as his friends, helping to partially fill the emptiness left in his life by, first, his early retirement and then the sudden death of his beloved wife.

In turn, Elrond Hubbard had impressed those around him with his educational knowledge and expertise, a rarity in an area blighted by its failing schools and poor attainment levels and high unemployment levels.

"I suppose it was only a matter of time before it happened," Nancy sighed, "As though fate was always meant to draw my father into their closed and secret circle."

"What happened?" Zach asked, noticing that the dark storm clouds had returned to Nancy's face.

"Don't get me wrong," she began, "It all appeared to be perfectly innocent to my father, to begin with."

Nancy glanced at a black and white photograph of a jovial looking man on her mantelpiece. "They asked him whether he would consider taking over as a *Super-Headteacher* - probably the first of its kind in this country - responsible for raising standards of teaching and learning in all the schools in St Godrics and the surrounding areas."

Dev struggled to suppress the image of a teacher wearing a mask and cape, with his underpants worn outside his trousers as Nancy continued to recount her father's life story.

She explained how the governors were extremely keen for her father to improve the prospects of the local children, especially those of their own offspring. However, Elrond Hubbard, though tremendously flattered, had politely, and repeatedly, declined the position, stating that his teaching days were long behind him.

"It was then that they dangled the one carrot in front of my father that could have ever changed his mind."

"Which was?" Zach asked eagerly.

Nancy sighed. "The opportunity to lay his eyes and hands on a book written secretly and exclusively for the author's friends and fellow Freemasons, known to but a handful of men as it secretly passed through history – whispered, but never acknowledged, its existence never, ever confirmed."

Zach could feel the tension rising in the room, his heart pounding in his throat as he awaited the next words to fall from Nancy Hubbard's lips.

"Roger Bacon's most mythical and infamous tome – *Educalis Totalis*. Or to call it by the name that all Freemasons know it by, *The Book of Absolute Knowledge*."

Chapter 15

Having initially arrived to discuss one mysterious book, Zach and his friends were taken aback to discover that Grammarticus wasn't even the most important tome in the lives of Elrond and Nancy Hubbard.

"The Book of Absolute Knowledge?" Shannon asked, struggling to comprehend Nancy's unexpected revelation.

"Yes," Nancy nodded, continuing, "Bacon was renowned, first and foremost, as a man of science, but his interests stretched further across many academic fields, a rare mind in a time when the world was a much smaller and superstitious place."

Nancy explained that Roger Bacon was a Franciscan friar who had lived back in the 13th century when he was also known by the name of *Doctor Mirabilis*.

"He was called by that name as a scholastic accolade, a way of showing how highly regarded and respected his theories and writings were," she explained, her eyes sparkling as she spoke, "Though commonly regarded as a philosopher and scholar, there were some who believed him to be a wizard or sorcerer after his creation of a *brazen head."*

Nancy continued to explain that a brazen head was a medieval automaton, or self-operating head, which was reputedly able to correctly answer any question put to it, though sometimes only by saying *Yes* or *No.*

"How would someone be able to create such technology so long ago?" Zach asked, scarcely believing what he was hearing.

Nancy shook her head and made to answer, but the

sound of Antonio snoring heavily, his head slumped against his ample chest, caused her to lose her focus momentarily.

"Tip your gran's head slightly to the side, dear," she quietly whispered to Kadija, "I often have to do that with my father."

Kadija nodded and lifted Antonio's head to tilt it slightly, ignoring the thin line of dribble which now ran down his wrinkled and whiskery chin.

"Now, where was I?" Nancy asked.

"The brazen head?" Dev urged, his shirt, trousers and underwear becoming sweatier and stickier with each passing second, "Zachariah asked how something like that could have been created so long ago?"

Nancy sighed and shook her head. "There is no actual, physical proof such a device ever existed. However, various historical recordings state that several people witnessed it being used and claim that Bacon actually used necromancy to create it."

"Necromancy? What's that?" Zach asked, not altogether sure that he really wanted to know the answer. When he heard Nancy's reply, he again wished he hadn't asked the question in the first place.

"Necromancy is the practice of dark magic," she stated, "It's where you communicate with the dead."

A cold chill seemed to fill the room, the eerie silence now punctuated only by the rattling sound that was coming from Antonio's sleeping form as Nancy continued her strange, but compelling, tale.

"At the time, it was believed that you could summon a spirit for various purposes and reasons – divination or foretelling the future; to use the dead as a weapon or, more likely in Bacon's case, asking them to impart the means to discover untold, secret and hidden knowledge."

Suddenly, a lightbulb lit up in Zach's brain as he began to join all of the dots together. "The brazen head that Bacon created wasn't a *literal* head was it?"

"Clever boy," Nancy smiled, "No, it was an *allegory*, a myth, a smokescreen and cover-story for his greatest secret - he'd used necromancy to help write and create his *magnum opus*, his masterpiece, *Educalis Totalis.*"

"Are you honestly telling us that a load of academic zombies," Shannon gulped, "supposedly helped Bacon when he was writing his book?"

Nancy smiled again as she shook her head. "No, nothing as quite as dramatic as that. But something mysterious did indeed happen. How else would Roger Bacon, a middle-aged monk of low-standing and little formal education, suddenly have the answers to any question ever asked of him?"

"So what type of spirits allegedly spoke to him?

"Philosophers, poets, mathematicians," Nancy replied, "At least, that's what he claimed. Either way, the *Educalis Totalis* was legendary, a book sought after by academics from all around the world. Often mentioned, but never truly believed to have ever existed, the secret property of the few and the privileged."

"Like your father's Freemason friends?" Zach said.

"Like my father's Freemason friends," Nancy repeated, "In return for him agreeing to take on the role they'd offered him, he was granted full and unhindered access to the book and its dark *'magical'* secrets."

Zach smiled to himself as Nancy used her fingers to emphasise invisible speech marks in the air when she said the word *'magical'*.

He silently wondered how fanciful the story would have sounded to those that had not recently experienced the bizarre and inexplicable events he and his friends had.

It seemed to Zach that the more Nancy retold her father's story, the more relieved she seemed to become in finally having others to listen without prejudice, not judging the truth of her tale, nor question her sanity when sharing it with them.

"At first," Nancy continued, "My father was so excited at the prospect of using the book. I can vividly remember the day he first brought it home."

Nancy used her head to gesture to the ceiling above her. "I was back from uni that week when, one night, he came in, clutching the book to his chest. It was tightly wrapped in ancient sackcloth to hide it from prying eyes, such as mine. My father quickly scurried upstairs, like a naughty schoolboy, and locked it in his study, safe and sound.

"Didn't he let you see it?" Kadija asked.

"Not at first," Nancy replied, smiling, "But as each night passed and the longer he spent pouring over its contents, the more I would go up to see him, using any excuse I could think of just to try to catch a glimpse of it."

Nancy explained that the tome itself looked just like any other medieval book of that period, bound in some battered and torn animal hide, its pages badly aged due to the river of time it had travelled just to exist in the present day and age.

Zach cast a worried look at his wristwatch, suddenly becoming more aware of the fact that they were losing the daylight and that he and his friends were still no nearer discovering a solution to their current problems.

However, he feared that were he to stop Nancy from sharing the history of Bacon's *Educalis Totalis*, then their one and only hope of breaking the spell that they'd unwittingly unleashed on their world would be lost to them forever.

"So when did Mr Hubbard write Grammarticus?" Zach asked, stopping Nancy, mid-flow.

"What? Oh, Grammarticus..." Nancy asked, her voice betraying itself, irritation masking every consonant and vowel that she now spoke. "It was only after my father had spent a month reading, analysing, digesting, almost dissecting every word written by Bacon that he finally accepted defeat in his quest to find the missing cypher code."

Nancy explained that no matter what combination of letters, numbers and sentences Hubbard had tried, he'd almost given up his efforts in unlocking Bacon's secret, the tome as mysterious and unreadable as it was from the very first moment he'd been given full and uninterrupted access to *Educalis Totalis*.

"Then, just when he had given up all hope..." Nancy said, glancing out across the hallway, pausing, like an actor, as though listening for a stage prompt from the wings. When one wasn't forthcoming, she continued. "Something unexpected happened. *Educalis Totalis* suddenly began to *speak* to him."

"*Speak* to him?" Shannon asked, looking at Zach.

"Speak to him," Nancy repeated, "To this day, my

father doesn't know how or why, but one night, *Educalis Totalis* just seemed to come alive in his head, guiding his hand, forcing him to write down all that it said to him."

The children sat and listened, transfixed, as Nancy recounted the events that led to the creation of Grammarticus. Well, all the children that is, except for Antonio, who continued to snore gently, his aged head now resting gently on the arm of the sofa, the material beneath it dark and damp from his drool. Nancy recalled how her father had suddenly awoken the next morning and sat bolt upright at his desk, the worn-out butts of numerous pencils discarded all around the floor of his study, a mountain of handwritten and pig-eared pages stacked beside him.

"He has no recollection of writing Grammarticus, from the minute that the book began to speak to him," Nancy said, "Until the final second that the last sheet of paper took its place at the end of his manuscript."

"What happened next?" Shannon asked, sensing that she already knew the answer, something that she knew her friends felt too.

"He went straight to school," Nancy replied, rubbing the end of her nose vigorously, "He somehow knew that he'd written something unique and important and was desperate to try it out. Little did he know how much his words would dramatically alter so many lives in such a short space of time, his and mine included."

The children listened intently as Nancy explained how her father had taken Grammarticus to school to teach a select band of children, those 'volunteered' by his Freemason friends, specially chosen because of birthright, not academic ability.

"The results were astonishing," Nancy continued, smiling wistfully, "Almost overnight, their spoken and written English dramatically improved, along with all their grammar, reading and comprehension skills and abilities. My father was ecstatic. He didn't know how Grammarticus had worked, but the students he taught seemed to bond with the book almost immediately."

"It spoke to them too, didn't it?" Dev asked, breaking his self-imposed silence, sniffing his armpits, which were pressed to his sides, in the process, his nose wrinkling in obvious disgust at the foul odour he'd undoubtedly smelt there.

"Yes, it did," Nancy sighed, seemingly oblivious to Dev's gesture, "Almost too much."

"Why do you say that?" Zach urged.

Nancy went to answer him but caught sight of the small, oak grandmother clock that hung on the wall behind him. "It's getting late, your parents must be expecting you home soon."

Shannon shook her head. "Not until we have all the answers we came for," she said determinedly, "Please do continue, Miss Hubbard."

The look that filled Nancy's face implied to Zach that she was a woman not used to being told what to do. She snorted moodily. "As I was saying, the initial results were so astonishing that my father called the members of his lodge to meet together to urgently discuss the ways he could reach even more children, giving them all unlimited access to Grammaticus."

Zach looked at Shannon and frowned. "How many more children?"

"Initially, all of the children who lived in St Godrics and the surrounding villages. Then, all those who lived in Cambridgeshire…"

Nancy paused for a moment before adding, "Before, finally, giving access to Grammarticus to all of the children of England."

"You don't mean..." Shannon began to ask in horror as Nancy slowly nodded her head.

"That's right, my father asked the Freemasons to produce and print hundreds and hundreds of copies of Grammarticus to send to every school up and down the country."

Chapter 16

It took Zach at least a minute or two to fully digest the stunning news that Nancy had just imparted on them all.

"Every school had its own copy of Grammarticus?" Shannon finally asked.

Nancy smiled and shook her head. "Fortunately not. For that, we actually have the Freemasons to thank."

Outside in the hallway, a whirring sound began in the room which housed Elrond Hubbard, as though reminding them that he was still very much a part of this story, despite his absence during its retelling.

"How come?" Chelsea-May asked, discreetly moving away from Dev, whose aroma was becoming much more pungent by the minute.

"They basically told my father that the book and its contents were just too valuable to be wasted on those not worthy of it," replied Nancy sadly, "The members of his lodge told him that the book should only be available to the great and the good. 'We can't just give an education to any old *riffraff*,' one Freemason told my father, 'We must preserve the natural, social order to keep the *peasants* in their place. There are those born to lead, and those meant to follow!'"

Shannon shot Zach a look before turning back to Nancy. "How did your father respond to that?"

"Badly," Nancy smiled, "As you can imagine, he was absolutely furious."

Outside, rain had begun to fall lightly, gently coating the windowpanes of the Old Rectory as Nancy detailed how Hubbard had argued long and hard, stating how disgusted he was that the opportunity to raise the education of millions of ordinary, working-class children was being denied to them by a small number of pompous, bigoted and middle-aged conservative men.

"Couldn't he just take Grammarticus and get it published himself?" Kadija asked, but Nancy had begun to shake her head before she had completed the question.

"He tried, of course, but the lodge told him that as he had used their copy of *Educalis Totalis* to create Grammarticus, then, by definition, the copyright of the book belonged to them."

Zach could almost picture the scene itself as Nancy detailed how her father had stormed off, leaving the manuscript with the lodge, vowing that he would go to the papers and tell them everything.

"It was only when they threatened to *advise* their friends who made up the board of trustees at my university," Nancy said sadly, "about how I had 'cheated' to obtain the grades needed to attend it that my father reluctantly agreed to stay quiet."

"Had you cheated?" Kadija asked innocently.

The look Nancy Hubbard shot in her direction spoke more than a thousand words ever could, Kadija mouthing an apology as she sank deeper into the depths of the sofa she sat on, no doubt finding numerous coins and items which had disappeared down its back and sides during its inanimate lifetime.

"What happened next?" Zach asked, attempting to draw Nancy's attention back to the sorry tale she told, whilst freeing Kadija from her steely glare.

"Nothing, initially," Nancy said, "He carried on as a

Super-Headteacher, doing his best to raise the standards in the schools he had been given the responsibility for."

The children listened silently as Hubbard's daughter recounted the frustrations that her father had felt from trying to raise the standards of the children in his charge, whilst denied the *'magic bullet'* he knew he had created in the form of Grammarticus.

"He tried to soldier on, but I could tell it was eating him up inside. In desperation, he made one final attempt to get the lodge to change their mind and allow Grammarticus to be shared once and for all."

"Did it work?" Zach asked, immediately kicking himself, already knowing what the next words to fall from Nancy's mouth would be."

"No, of course not," Nancy replied, adding, "They simply dismissed him from the lodge instead."

Nancy continued to tell them how the Freemasons had told Hubbard that they had arranged for a small, print run of the book that they wanted to trial with a select band of graduates, teachers and academics, who would then be tasked with testing Grammarticus on a number of privileged students who then would become 'the future leaders of our great country.'

"'After all,' one of them taunted as my father left the lodge for a final time, 'You must know that you won't ever be able to tell a decent *story* in this country without having a *Tory* in it!'"

Chelsea-May frowned angrily. "What a bunch of low-life, no good bas-"

"Language, young lady!" the elderly figure of Antonio spat, having suddenly sat bolt upright, his face squashed and red from where he'd been laying.

Nancy laughed. "I called them far worse than that when my father told me, trust me, dear!"

"So what did Mr Hubbard do to stop them?" Zach pressed gently.

"What any good author would do if their work was stolen," Nancy smiled, "He broke into the lodge and stole it back!"

Where, previously, the room had been silent, save the recollections of the pretty middle-aged woman, now it echoed with the laughter of a half-dozen young children – that's if you included Antonio, of course.

"Seriously?" Zach asked once the furore had died down again.

"Absolutely," Nancy replied, "He broke in through a back window and took back Grammarticus from under their noses."

"What did they do?"

"Nothing. They didn't even contact the police."

"Why ever not?" Shannon snapped, her desire to know the complete story getting the better of her and her manners.

"Isn't it obvious," Zach said, resting a calming hand on her knee, "They didn't need it as they already had their own copies, didn't they Miss Hubbard?"

"Yes they did," Nancy agreed, adding, "Still, my father took the precaution of immediately hiding the original copy of the book, as he expected to receive a visit from either the Freemasons or the police, demanding its immediate return," Nancy replied, "But none were forthcoming. Not the next day, nor the next week. In fact, he was left to carry on as though nothing untoward had ever happened…" she paused, her tongue darting to moisten her lips, "Initially."

"What do you mean," Shannon urged, "'Initially'?"

"My, you're a feisty one, aren't you?" Nancy laughed, "It was about a month later that my father received a phone call, from the man who had first invited him to join the lodge – I can't for the life of me remember his name though. Anyway, he asked my father to meet with him. Told him that it was in both of their interests and, ultimately mine as well, that he attend."

"What did your father do?" Zach asked, feeling that Nancy's, and Elrond Hubbard's tale, was about to reach its final, dramatic conclusion."

"He went, of course."

Outside, the rain was now beating much more heavily against the windows of the living room, the late early evening sky having darkened enough for Nancy to stand and flick the light switch on, glancing out into the hallway as the rest of the downstairs gradually became bathed in soft light.

"Dad phoned me shortly before he left," Nancy said, taking her seat again, "I warned him against it but, as usual, my father knew best…"

Zach, Shannon and the others listened as Nancy began to vividly paint the scene, obviously having inherited some of her father's storytelling talents. They almost felt as though they were travelling back in time themselves as Nancy explained how Elrond Hubbard had driven through St Godrics, back to the school he had so desperately wanted to help in the first place.

Nancy explained that the school building itself was pitch black when he arrived, the only light present being that of the full moon which hung high in the clear, night sky above him.

However, Hubbard had the presence of mind to retrieve a flashlight from the boot of his car before he began to make his way around the building, searching out the man who had asked to secretly meet with him at such a late hour.

"Eventually, Nancy continued, "My father arrived in the grassed area between the two wings of the school which was normally reserved for the eating of packed lunches as well as other any general outdoor learning activities. There was no sign of his friend, so my father turned to leave. That's when he first caught sight of it."

"Caught sight of what?" Antonio shouted, his shrill old woman's voice piercing the eerie silence that had wrapped itself around them all.

"He wasn't sure at first," Nancy said sadly, "But, then, when it cried so plaintively, it left my father in no doubt that whatever it was, it wasn't human and was obviously in a great deal of pain."

Zach could tell by the sorrowful expression Nancy's face wore that it pained her to relive the events of so long ago. He watched as she took another small sip of water before explaining how her father had slowly moved towards the shadows of one of the buildings toward the source of the sound he'd heard.

She told them that her father had bent down to find a small body covered in hair. At first, Hubbard had thought it a cat or a dog, but when the animal began to bleat faintly as he touched it, he soon realised that it was a young goat - a kid – and it appeared to be in a great amount of pain and distress.

"As soon as my father felt its body," Nancy

continued, "He could feel the blood on its coat, his fingers sticky to the touch. It was obvious to him that the animal was badly injured."

"What did he do?" Kadija asked anxiously, her stomach twisting into multiple knots, disgusted by the thought that anyone would ever cause such harm to another living creature, let alone one so young and defenceless.

"At first, thinking that the kid had been attacked by a fox," Nancy continued, "my father just gently lifted its head. He feared that if he moved it too much, he might cause it greater injury. That's when he saw *it* glint in the light of his torch."

"Saw what glint?" Zach pressed.

Nancy sighed. "The knife. Stupidly, my father picked it up, not quite believing what he now held. That's exactly how they found him."

"Who found him?"

"The police who had suddenly appeared from nowhere," Nancy replied, coldly, "And who just happened to have a reporter and a photographer there with them at the school late that night!"

Chapter 17

Zach felt as though he'd had all of the wind knocked out of him. Everything he had been told, or thought that he knew, about Elrond Hubbard was a lie. Hubbard wasn't the villain here - he was the victim!

"My father spent the night in the police cells, protesting his innocence," Nancy said sadly, "But it was no good. They charged him with animal cruelty and released him on bail, pending prosecution. He went home, distraught, a broken man."

Zach felt an incredible sense of guilt as he silently listened as Nancy explained how her father had immediately been suspended by the governors of the school and how he was shunned by all and sundry, friends he had recently made walking by him in the street, as well as refusing to take his telephone calls.

"I offered to come home," Nancy continued, "But he again refused, saying that there was no point in ruining both of our lives. How I wish I'd ignored him and come home immediately. If I'd been here when *they* came to see him, then maybe things would have worked out differently and I would still have *that* version of my father, not the shell of a man he is now."

"Who came to see him?" Zach asked, aware of the anger that Nancy had felt when she spat out her words earlier.

Nancy sighed, composing herself again. "It was about three weeks later. My father was at home, trying to keep himself busy so as to not fall into one of the black moods that dogged him so after his arrest, when there was a knock at the door. Had my father not had the foresight to install CCTV because of what had happened to him at the school that fateful night, then I would have had no knowledge of the events that unfolded here that day. When he went to the door, he opened it to find the man who had first introduced him to the lodge, along with a much younger looking woman."

"What did they want?"

"Grammarticus, of course."

Shannon shook her head, unsure as to what she was hearing. "But why did they need Grammarticus? Didn't they still have their own copies of the book?"

"Yes they did," Nancy nodded, a small smile now creasing her lips, "Only they had a little bit of a problem with them…"

As Zach listened to Nancy explain how her father had reluctantly let his unwelcomed guests cross the threshold of his home, he suddenly became aware of some movement from the corner of his eye.

He glanced into the hallway and caught sight of a frail, old man, sat on a motorised scooter, sitting in the doorway of the room at the end of the hall.

The image of Elrond Hubbard brought to mind that of the legendary physicist Stephen Hawking, so similar were the vehicles that housed their broken bodies. Hubbard appeared to be listening intently as his daughter explained how the man and woman had again asked him to hand over his original copy of the book.

Despite his twisted and contorted frame, Zach could sense by the softness in Hubbard's eyes a fierce intelligence that had been cruelly trapped in a useless body.

"My father laughed in their faces, of course," Nancy continued, "not understanding how desperate they were for the original book, even though they already had multiple copies of their own. It was only when the woman began to explain that there were '*issues*' with their books, that my father realised just how desperate the lodge was to have the original copy."

"Issues?" Shannon asked, "What sort of issues can a book have?"

"Maybe the pages started to become unstuck," Chelsea-May replied, "My mum's trashy, romance novels always fall apart when we go on holiday. The sun melts the glue that binds them together or something."

"If it had been something as simple as that," Nancy said, "Then they would have just got their copies re-bound. No, this was much more serious, something that defied logic, something, dare I say, magical and mysterious."

"How so?"

"Words, sentences and entire passages were simply disappearing from the text, just fading away…"

From the corner of his eye Zach again noticed the faintest of movements as Hubbard's motorised chair slowly inched its way out of the doorway as Nancy revealed that the copies of Grammarticus the lodge possessed were rapidly losing all of the text that was copied from Hubbard's original tome, the pages becoming as blank as the day that they were first created.

"Naturally, my father again refused to give up his copy of the book," Nancy said, adding, "Which caused the woman to lose her temper with him, hurling abuse and vile insults in his direction."

"Did that intimidate him?" Shannon asked.

"Oh no, on the contrary," Nancy smiled, "It only served to make him more determined not to give up his book. And, just for good measure, he told the man and the woman that he knew exactly why the words were disappearing and what could be done for them to still read their copies of the book."

"Did he really know how to read words that aren't there?" Zach said, suddenly feeling renewed hope at being able to resolve their own desperate situation. Nancy shrugged her shoulders. "Who knows. All I know is that the man stepped in and offered my father a deal – his copy of Grammarticus in return for all charges to be dropped against him and his immediate reinstatement to his position as Super-Headteacher."

I know what I'd have done had I been in his position, Zach thought as Nancy looked out and smiled at her father who now sat, motionless, looking back at her.

"True to form, my father refused," she said sadly, adding, "saying the last words that I've ever heard him say naturally, albeit recorded on videotape."

"Which were?" Shannon pressed.

"I remember seeing Dad on the grainy CCTV video footage a few days later, that defiant and mischievous look he used to have plastered all over his face as he uttered them – 'You think that just by offer my job back to me in return for the book you wanted me to write will be enough? Frankly, I'm lost for words, speechless in fact!'"

Nancy's voice faltered momentarily before she continued, "It was then that he collapsed, apparently having suffered something similar to a massive stroke, though we've never, ever discovered quite what it was. Whatever it was though, he hasn't spoken a single word without his voice simulator since that day."

Nancy turned to look out at her father, the love that she felt for him there for all to see. "I lost the father I had always known that day. There are some, rare moments when I can still see him, lost somewhere behind his eyes. Trapped. But the razor-sharp mind, his amazing memory, full of facts, figures and useless information was wiped out in an instant. Occasionally I get a glimpse of the man that he used to be but those moments lessen with each passing day."

Zach thought that he spotted a brief change in Hubbard's facial features but put it down to wishful thinking as Nancy concluded her story, detailing how the man and woman had first called the emergency services, before leaving abruptly once the paramedics had eventually arrived.

In time, the hospital had called her at university to explain the severity of her father's condition.

"That was the last we ever heard from the lodge," Nancy said bitterly, "Except for a letter a few weeks later which stated that although he had had been suspended from school and was to be relieved of his position, as an act of good faith due to his life-changing illness, they would award him a 'golden handshake', a one-off, lump sum payment."

"That seems a bit odd," Shannon said, "Why ever would they do that?"

"The letter said it was to thank him for his lifetime service and dedication to education and to help pay for his future medical needs, as well as providing him with a generous pension to see out his days," Nancy replied, "But, in truth, I believe it to be hush-money, a way of buying my continued silence, especially after I'd contacted the lodge to say that I'd viewed the hidden CCTV footage. Of course, it would mean nothing to anyone else as they hadn't said anything that could prove that they had set my father up. But they now knew that I knew about that damned book too. That was the last that we ever heard from them, and of Grammarticus, until your phone call today." Hubbard's daughter leant forward, resting her elbows on her knees and fixed Zach with a steely look, somehow sensing that he was the one who held all the answers. "So, having heard the truth behind Grammarticus' tawdry history, please do me the same courtesy - what are your *real* reasons for coming here today? But, more importantly, explain to me exactly how and why you think my father, given his current condition, could possibly help you and your friends?"

"…and that's honestly the truth as to why we are all here today," Zach concluded, "We were hoping that you and your father would know a way of undoing whatever Grammarticus is causing to happen."
Zach glanced at Shannon hopefully, noticing the time on the clock behind Dev.
Twenty minutes, he thought, *that's all it's taken me to detail the chaos and mayhem that has happened in the past few weeks ever since we found that blasted book!*
Shannon smiled back at him, reassuring Zach that he had explained the situation as well as he could, none of his friends having interjected or contradicted his

long recount of events.

An air of expectation briefly hung around them, only for it to be swept away again as Nancy suddenly stood, sweeping her hands down the front of her skirt, smoothing away the creases that had formed there whilst sitting.

"I'm sorry to disappoint you, but it's been a wasted journey then," Nancy said, turning to look at her father, who was now moving slowly towards her, "As far as I'm concerned, that chapter of our lives closed long ago," she placed a hand on the shoulder of the frail old man who now sat, blocking the doorway.

"Please, Miss Hubbard," Zach asked as he stood, all of his friends – bar Antonio, who'd drifted off to sleep again – mirroring the gesture, "You're the only ones who could possibly help end all this."

Nancy looked down at her father, who was slowly typing one letter at a time with an index finger on his keypad, before she turned back to the six of them.

"Look, until today, I didn't know that cursed book still existed. Even if there was a way to help you, I simply wouldn't know how," Nancy sighed, "I'm really sorry, but I'm going to have to ask you to leave. It's already way past my father's tea-time. Can't you see how agitated he is? No doubt I'm going to be told off any minute now-"

"NO..." the now familiar mechanical voice boomed as Elrond Hubbard's voice simulator translated the words that he slowly typed," WE... MUST... HELP...THE...CHILDREN... NONE... OF... THIS...IS...THEIR... FAULT... WE... HAVE... TO...PUT...THIS...ALL...RIGHT...AGAIN"

"But, Dad," Nancy pleaded, "I wouldn't know where

to start even if I wanted too!"

Hubbard sighed deeply before he turned his wheelchair towards Zach and Shannon, typing as quickly as his frail body would allow him too, the great effort needed etched on his lined and aged face. "THE...DAY... I... LOST... MY... VOICE..." he began, sweat now beginning to form on his brow, "WAS...THE... VERY...SAME...DAY...THAT... GRAMMARTICUS...LOST...ITS...VOICE...TOO ...IT... HAS... SPOKEN... TO... YOU... AND... YOU... ALONE...ITS...CHOSEN...YOU...TO... BE...ITS...VOICE...AGAIN..."

Zach took an involuntary step back as the old headteacher slowly began to trundle forwards, stopping only a matter of inches away from him.

"If that's all true," Zach finally asked, "Then how do I get it to listen to me and stop everything that's happening?"

Elrond Hubbard smiled as he typed, his eyes seeming to twinkle as he stared up and Zach and Shannon. "TO... END... ITS... CURSE..." his robotic voice droned, "YOU... MUST...SIMPLY...READ... BETWEEN...THE... LINES..."

"But there's hardly any text left in the book for us to infer or interpret," Shannon argued, but Hubbard had already begun to turn his wheelchair around to leave the room again.

"READ...BETWEEN... THE... LINES..." his artificial voice repeated, "I...THINK...THAT...I... WOULD...LIKE...SOME...FISH...AND CHIPS... FOR...MY...TEA...PLEASE...NANCY..."

The children stood in stunned silence and watched as Hubbard slowly trundled back into the hallway before disappearing into his room again.

Zach looked pleadingly at Nancy, who just shrugged her shoulders in resignation.

"See," she said sadly, "Even if I wanted to help, I couldn't. As you have just seen for yourselves, my father's mind simply isn't what it used to be. He often talks in riddles, just like that."

Nancy glanced out of her window before her eyes again fell on the disconsolate faces of the children before her. "Look, as it's getting late, let me run you all home. It's the very least that I can do."

It had gone past seven o'clock by the time that Nancy's specially converted people carrier pulled up outside of Shannon's house.

Inside, only Zach and Shannon remained, their friends having been dropped off at their respective homes en route – that was after the two toilet breaks needed for Antonio to empty his prematurely geriatric bladder.

As the two children stood on the pavement, Nancy rolled down her car window and looked at Zach. "Are you sure you don't want me to run you back home as well, it's really no trouble?"

Zach shook his head. "No, I'm good, thanks. I'll walk from here. Thanks for everything, Miss Hubbard."

"It's Nancy," Nancy frowned, continuing, "I'm really sorry we couldn't have been more help. I hope it all works out for you; I really do. Well, I suppose I'd better text my father to let him know that I'm on my way back home via the chippy. He can get quite crotchety when he's *hangry*!"

Shannon smiled as she watched Nancy reach into her

handbag and pull out her mobile phone before turning to Zach. "So, what do we do now?"

Zach shook his head. "I don't know, Shan. All I know is that I can't face another minute, let alone another week of this. Plus, there's the small matter of Miss Fletcher that we still have to contend with! Can you even begin to imag-"

"Fletcher?" Nancy suddenly interrupted, her head snapping back up as she looked at them, "Did you say, *Fletcher*?"

"Yes," Shannon said, "Miss Fletcher, our wicked witch of a teacher! Why do you ask?"

"Oh, it's probably nothing," Nancy replied, tossing her phone onto the passenger seat as she let down the handbrake, "It's just that I'm pretty sure that was the surname of the man who first introduced my father to the lodge."

Shannon and Zach stared, open-mouthed as Nancy sped off, waving a hand at them through the car window as she drove away.

"Zach...you don't think..." Shannon began to ask.

"With everything else that's happened recently," Zach replied, "I most certainly do! The question now is what's going to happen next?"

"Well, there's only one way to find out," Shannon replied as she walked up the steps which led to her front door, "However, we need to get our hands on Grammarticus more urgently than ever."

Zach shook his head. "There's no way they'll let us in the library when we go back to school on Monday."

Shannon inserted her key in the door lock and turned it before looking at Zach, a naughty and mischievous grin rapidly crept across her face. "Who said we had to wait until then?"

"I'm not sure I follow, Shan." Zach replied before suddenly realising just what his friend was implying, "You're not really suggesting…"

"Oh yes, absolutely," Shannon smiled as she pushed the door open before her. "If we break into the school library tomorrow, we won't need to ask anyone's permission, will we?"

Chapter 18

"I can't believe you actually talked me into this," Chelsea-May moaned the following morning, "I had to pretend I was sick so I could avoid going to Sunday service. If they ever find out that I was here, I'll be grounded for a week."

Dev put a reassuring hand on his friend's shoulder, causing Chelsea-May to wince slightly from the smell of his armpit. "I wouldn't go worrying too much about that," he whispered, "Trust me - if we're caught, that will be the least of our worries."

Zach tried to smile as he looked at his friends, who had gathered in the park which adjoined the school grounds with him early that day.

What they planned to do was ridiculous.

How they looked was ridiculous, each of them dressed from head to foot in black, wearing either balaclavas, baseball caps or scarves to try and cover their features and, hopefully, conceal their true identities.

All except Antonio that was, who had taken off one of his grandmother's support stockings and pulled it tightly over his head, squashing his nose against his elderly cheek, making him look like a geriatric bank robber!

"You needn't have dressed up, Antonio," Zach said gently as Dev carefully began to cut the wire fence that separated the park from the school playground, "You can always stay here and be a look-out."

"Nonsense, young man!" Antonio replied, now sounding exactly like his Nonna, "I'm coming with you...but I need to go for a piddle first."

Kadija and Shannon had to suppress the urge to laugh as Antonio disappeared behind the nearest bush.

"There!" Dev said triumphantly as the wire fence yielded before him, "We're in."

As Dev put his dad's wire-cutters back in his holdall and emptied the contents of another can of body spray over himself, Zach gathered his friends into a huddle, including Antonio, who had returned, a faint whiff of wee accompanying him.

"Right, this is it," Zach whispered, "You all know your roles?"

Everybody nodded, recalling the detailed instructions that they'd received by text from Zach and Shannon the night before.

"Remember to position yourselves at regular look-out points between here and the library," Shannon added, "If you see anyone or anything suspicious, then make the sound of a bird to the person nearest you."

Kadija raised her hand. "What type of bird sound? I'm not very good at animal impersonations."

Zach sighed. "Whatever bird sound you can do will be fine, just as long as the next person can clearly hear you and relay any message to me and Shannon in the library..."

"So, a chicken then?"

"What?"

"A chicken. I can do a wicked impression of a chicken."

Zach shook his head. "I don't think a chicken would really be appropriate, Kadge."

"No, you're probably right," Kadija frowned as she watched as Shannon crawled through the fence in front of her, "How about a goose?"

"How many geese have you seen around the school?" Zach replied, trying hard to conceal his frustration as he and Dev held the fence up for Antonio to slowly crawl through, giving them both an eyeful of his Nonna's belly-warming knickers as he did so.

"Man! That's way too much information!" Dev moaned as Chelsea-May crouched down to follow suit.

"Perhaps a woodpecker then," Kadija whispered as she watched her friend ease her way through the small gap, Chelsea-May's hoody snagging the fence in the process.

"Yes! Thank God!" Zach sighed.

"Ha-ha-ha-ha-ha," Kadija sang as she climbed through the fence, *"Ha-ha-ha-ha-ha! Ha-ha-ha-ha-ha -HAAAAA HA!"*

"A real one, Kadge," Zach snapped, "Not Woody, the flipping woodpecker off the TV!"

"Look on the bright side, Zach," Dev smiled as he climbed through the fence after her, "Things can only get better."

Well, they can't be any worse than how you smell, my friend, Zach thought, holding his breath as he crawled on his hands and knees after Dev before quickly following the others as they all crept across the deserted playground…

But the scene which greeted Zach and Shannon when they finally reached the library proved that things could get a whole lot worse.

Far worse.

And had.

"They've totally gutted it!" Shannon gasped as she

stared through the window to the side of the library, "There's nothing left in there at all!"

Zach peered through the glass in disbelief, his mind desperately trying to make sense of the barren sight before them.

Where row upon row of giant bookcases filled with books, like trees of knowledge, had previously stood, now there was just a desert of dust.

The entire room had been stripped bare, devoid of anything, except the dust sheets, tools and equipment abandoned by the workmen brought in to quell the sudden bookworm infestation.

Even the walls themselves had nothing but a sickly hue, covered by some sort of foam the workmen had liberally coated over their surface, leaving them looking as though they were waiting to be shaved by a demonic barber.

"They've gutted the entire library," Zach finally managed to say, his voice choked with emotion.

"Sadly, they had no choice," a familiar voice said from behind where Zach and Shannon stood, their noses pressed hard against the dusty windowpane.

The two children turned and looked up into the face of Mr Copthorne before realising that Kadija, Dev, Chelsea-May and Antonio were closely stood beside him.

"Mr Copthorne found us looking for the football," Dev said, raising his eyebrows behind the burly site manager, hoping that Zach or Shannon would pick up on the cover-story that they'd spun Mr Copthorne.

"That's right," Mr Copthorne added gruffly, "Though why you couldn't have just left it for school tomorrow is beyond me."

"That's because of Antonio's Nonna," Chelsea-May chipped in, "She bought back a football from Italy as a surprise gift for him and wanted us to test it out for her before she gives it to Antonio."

Mr Copthorne frowned as he looked at *Nonnantonio*. "Testing out a football? They're all the ruddy same!" Chelsea-May looked at Dev, desperate for some help and moral support.

"Not this one," Dev said, "It simply flew over the fence into the school grounds after I kicked it. It's made from the finest Italian leather, you see. There isn't a football anywhere in the world that swerves, bounces and rolls so well."

Mr Copthorne again looked sceptically at the old woman. "Is that right, *Signora...*"

"*Si,*" Antonio replied, "*Molto bella!*"

"Very beautiful," Shannon added, translating the only Italian her friend knew fluently, "And very expensive it was too! We simply had to go look for it as Antonio's grandmother was getting most upset."

"That so," Mr Copthorne asked, again staring at Antonio, who was now doing his best *hangdog* impression as he sadly nodded back at the site manager.

"Yes, Mr Copthorne," Shannon nodded, "We crawled through a gap we found cut in the fence..."

"...then split up to cover as much ground as we could to search for the football," Zach continued.

"Must have been a helluva kick if you think it would have ended up in there!" Mr Copthorne said, gesturing at the desolate library behind them.

Shannon and Zach looked back at the library window, then toward the site manager.

"No," Shannon laughed, "We were just stunned to see the library looking the way it is."

Mr Copthorne shook his head. "As I said before, the workmen had no option but to gut it all. The moth infestation was just too severe. There was no other option but to toss the lot and start again."

"The lot," Zach repeated, "As in…"

"Carpets, furnishings, bookcases and books, sadly."

Zach let out an audible groan and fell to his knees, his heart and hopes sinking almost as much as his body just had.

Mr Copthorne appeared to be genuinely taken aback. "You surprise me, Zach! I thought you'd be pleased?" he said, adding, "After all, it gets you out of having to spend any more time sorting that mess of a library out, doesn't it?"

"It does," Shannon replied, "But we were really enjoying rummaging through the banned book section. It's not every day you get to read such rare and obscure works of literature."

"And now we'll never have the chance again," Zach added dejectedly.

"Not necessarily," Mr Copthorne winked, "Follow me."

Zach and Shannon looked at the others as the site manager pulled a large ring of keys out of a pocket in his overalls and began to walk off past the library, towards one of the areas normally restricted to pupils and parents of the school.

The six children hurriedly followed, each of them taking three strides for every one of Mr Copthorne's as he approached some temporary fencing which had been put up around four bright, yellow skips. Each skip was full to the brim with the ruined contents of the library.

Zach's eyes lit up as Mr Copthorne fumbled to find the right key to unlock a padlock to release the chain that held two of the fences together.

"I shouldn't really be doing this," the site manager whispered as he unravelled the chain and pulled open one of the fences, "But they're only going to be incinerated tomorrow. Just don't let on to any of the other children about this, OK?"

"Of course not," Zach said as he headed towards the skip before suddenly stopping to look back at the kindly site manager. "You won't lose your job for giving away the books, will you?"

Mr Copthorne began to laugh loudly. "Good God, no! The books are useless as they are, so they're fair game for anyone who wants them!"

"That's OK then," Zach smiled as he and the others turned and looked at the daunting task before them.

"No, there's no chance of that," Mr Copthorne continued as the children gingerly began to probe the books that were jutting out from the skip at all angles, "Especially after your teachers have had a good rummage through them already!"

Shannon and Zach stopped in their tracks and looked back at the site manager, who stood watching, hands now shoved deep into his pockets as he rocked back and forth on his heels.

"The teachers have already had a look themselves?" Shannon asked, a sudden feeling of fear and dread overwhelming her.

"Yep," Mr Copthorne replied, "They all had a good rifle through the skips yesterday afternoon. Even that *hoity-toity* Miss Fletcher came in and had a good nose about in them."

Zach swallowed hard. "Really?"

"Yep, she didn't get much though as most of the other teachers had already got the best of the books by the time she eventually arrived."

Hope sprang again in Zach's heart, only for it to soon be slammed back into the ground and trampled underfoot by Mr Copthorne's very next sentence.

"Mind you, she did seem pretty ecstatic with a battered and beaten old book that she scurried off with at the end of the afternoon…"

Chapter 19

The three of them couldn't quite put their fingers on it, but there was definitely something different about Miss Fletcher during their Grammar and English lessons the following Monday morning.

Zach, Shannon and **Kadija** had nervously taken their seats as the wizened, skeletal figure harangued and belittled the children in front of them in her usual, cynical manner, Miss Fletcher's words clipped and cutting, aiming barb after barb at the children before her.

As usual.

Only this time, there was something else.

Something about the way she stood...

Something about the way she talked...

Something about the way she smelt...

Something...*off.*

Zach and his friends couldn't be certain but Miss Fletcher appeared to be even more arrogant, more contemptuous, with a greater air of superiority about her than ever before as she looked through her spectacles and down her nose at the terrified pupils who were entrusted to her daily care by trusting parents.

All through the lesson, they watched transfixed as Miss Fletcher seemed to glide across the room, destroying egos, crushing young hopes and expectations, savaging the work of those that had done their very best to please her.

Sometimes during their previous lessons, the cold and unpleasant teacher would seem to recognise when she had totally overstepped the mark and slightly soften her tone, especially with those considered as the chosen ones – her favourites.

But not today.

Everyone was fair game as Miss Fletcher took aim and character-assassinated them all, seemingly with little care for their feelings or the consequences of her cruel deeds, words and actions.

That's it, Zach suddenly thought, *she just doesn't care anymore! Now that she has Grammarticus she thinks she needn't bother teaching us, that somehow the book will do it for her. How wrong could she be*?

But there was something else though.

Something that he and the others glimpsed, albeit, only occasionally.

A hint.

A whisper.

A tease.

There was now a new malevolence surrounding the mysterious enigma of Miss Fletcher that they couldn't quite fathom or work out.

Not yet, anyway.

"Right, you miserable, illiterate rabble of riffraff!" the deputy-headteacher roared at the end of their lesson, "You'd better get lively. Things are soon going to change around here. Anyone not willing or able to keep up had better prepare themselves for a different set..."

Zach couldn't be certain, but he thought he heard Miss Fletcher then mutter, "Or, preferably, a different school and county," as she turned to wipe the board, before ending her tirade with, "Class, dismissed."

Shannon and Kadija stood by the door waiting for their friend, casually casting their eyes around the

classroom, hoping to catch sight of Grammaticus.
"There!" Kadija whispered triumphantly, pointing
behind Shannon as Zach finally joined them. He
followed the line that her finger took until his eyes
fell on the leather-bound book which rested on the
top-shelf of Miss Fletcher's built-in cupboard in the
corner of the classroom.

A cupboard whose door they watched as it was slid-
shut and locked by their nemesis.

Miss Fletcher turned and looked the three of them
squarely in the eyes, her tightly drawn lips creasing
into a yellowed, gap-toothed grin.

"Haven't you all got somewhere else you're supposed
to be like, say, the library?" she barked, before
adding, "Oh, silly me! I meant to say, *ex-library*!"

Zach, Shannon and Kadija couldn't be certain, but
Miss Fletcher seemed to smile knowingly as she
dramatically dropped the key into her handbag.

"Not that low-life like you would know what to do
given unlimited time spent in and around endless
knowledge and wisdom," she laughed, storming past
the three of them, cackling loudly as she scurried
down the corridor.

"God, I really hate her!" Kadija said once Miss
Fletcher was safely out of earshot, "I'd like to give
her a piece of my-"

"Kadge, no!" Zach yelled, slapping a hand across his
friend's mouth, "You know what happens when we
are too literal!"

"Zach's right," Shannon agreed as Zach slowly
lowered his hand, "We have to be really careful about
what we say and how we say it. At least until we can
get hold of that book that is."

"That's going to be easier said than done," Kadija replied, "You saw how she looked at us – it's so painfully obvious that she suspects that we know something about Grammarticus."

"True," Zach replied, pulling his mobile phone from his pocket, "She must have her suspicions by now, but I don't think that she fully knows the whole truth about us and it."

"Won't take her long to work it out though, will it?" Shannon shook her head. "No, it won't, Kadge. That's why we need to get the book tonight."

"We can't wait until then," said Zach, his words obscured by the tongue that he now clenched firmly between his teeth as he frantically typed on his phone screen, "We get it now!"

Shannon and Kadija stared at each other. "And how do you propose we do that?" Kadija moaned, "Are you going to kick the door down like they do in those awful action films?"

"Better than that," Zach smiled, holding up his phone in triumph, "I've summoned reinforcements!"

It was another ten minutes by the time that Chelsea-May and Dev arrived at Miss Fletcher's classroom door, the remnants of her lunch still clinging to the edges of Chelsea-May's lips, Dev's shirt stuck tightly to his skin, its material as wet and stinky as an old and used dishcloth.

Shannon and Kadija still couldn't work out how this was going to make their task any easier as they closed the classroom door and followed Zach and Dev to the cupboard.

"I'll keep a lookout," Chelsea-May said, producing a

doughnut for her pocket, picking some trouser lint off it before forcing most of it into her mouth.

"Gross!" Kadija moaned as she returned her attention to the boy who was knelt before the cupboard door.

It was only when Dev pulled a strange looking set of keys from his back-pocket that she remembered that Dev had - *ahem* – other talents.

Hidden talents.

Illegal talents.

"Not often I get the chance to do this nowadays," Dev said as he slid one of his skeleton-key set into the lock on the cupboard door, "Have had to keep a low profile since the last time...social worker's orders!"

Zach and the others watched in awe as Dev twisted his hand first one way, then another, the sound of metal on metal assaulting their ears as he furiously worked the lock.

"It's no use," Kadija moaned, "There's no way that lock is ever going to-"

Click.

"Famous last words," Dev smiled as he stood again, "Voila!"

Dev slowly slid open the cupboard door to reveal Grammarticus sat on the shelf in front of them.

"All we have to do now is grab the book," Zach said, stepping into the cupboard, "And get it to Antonio."

"How are we going to do that?" Shannon asked.

"Simple," Zach replied, lifting the book, "We'll toss it out the window. Antonio should be outside, waiting for us to drop it to him."

"There he is!" Chelsea-May beamed, waving at the ancient figure of Antonio stood on the grass below the classroom, "Our getaway granny!"

Shannon laughed before suddenly stopping and frowning. "Weren't you supposed to be keeping a look-out, Chelsea-May?"

"Yeah, but I got bored of doing that, so I came to see how you lot were getting on instead."

"So who's watching the classroom door now then?" Zach asked, anxiously.

"No one!" an all-too-familiar voice screeched from behind them, "Give me that book!"

The children turned to stare into the eyes of Miss Fletcher, her face red with rage as she barred their exit from the classroom.

"I knew it! I knew that you runts were up to something," the teacher snarled, "But I couldn't quite work out what. Now I know - you found *my* book in the library, didn't you?"

"Yes, we did," Zach said defiantly, "And we're going to undo all that we've done before destroying it forever."

"I don't think so, give it to me now!" Miss Fletcher boomed, extending a palm towards the terrified children, who were now all huddled together.

"You can't make us!" Kadija taunted.

"I said NOW!" Miss Fletcher screamed, thrusting her hand out before her in a clawed, grabbing gesture. Suddenly, the book ripped itself from Zach's grip and began to levitate toward the teacher, as though suspended on strings by a giant, unseen puppeteer.

It was hard to determine who was more visibly shocked - the children at seeing the book being invisibly taken from them or Miss Fletcher who, realising that she was the one causing the book to gently float toward her, began to coax it along more quickly with her talon-like index finger.

"Well, I never! Fancy that!" the teacher beamed as Grammarticus drew nearer to her outstretched hand. Without thought or warning, Dev made a last-ditch attempt to snatch it from her, sweatily sailing through the air in the book's direction, but Miss Fletcher quickly pointed her other hand at the flailing pupil. A flash of green, like a lightning bolt, erupted from her fingertips, hitting Zach squarely in the chest, causing him to disintegrate immediately, the only sign of Dev ever existing being the pile of ash his remains formed on the ground below.

"Ooh, I like this!" Miss Fletcher cackled as she stared at her hands, Grammarticus now suspended in mid-air halfway between the teacher and the terrified children.

Zach stared at the mound of dust that was once his friend in stunned silence as the three girls around him burst into tears.

"You've murdered Dev!" Kadija screamed, Shannon having slumped to the floor beside her.

"It would appear so," Miss Fletcher grinned, her eyes never leaving her hands as she turned them over, as though seeing them for the very first time, "How marvellous!"

"You're a cruel, mean and evil old woman!" Chelsea-May cried, throwing the last remains of her half-eaten doughnut at Miss Fletcher.

"Better that than being a big, fat pig, my dear!" Miss Fletcher smiled, flexing the fingers on her left hand.

"No!" Kadija shouted, but it was too late as she watched Chelsea-May first *yelp*, then *oink*, then *squeal* as she ran as fast as her trotters could carry her little pink body out through the classroom door.

"I just knew you were all too thick and ignorant to have done that well in your SATs tests. I was certain you'd somehow managed to cheat them," Miss Fletcher said, twirling Grammarticus around and around in the air, "But I wasn't sure how. Now it's all so painfully obvious - you found this book. And I suspect, by your apparent desperation to reclaim it, you also know of Grammarticus' naughty little secret, don't you?"

"Yes," Kadija snarled, "And you'll get what's coming to you when we get our hands back on it!"

"Oh, do shut up," yawned Miss Fletcher, clicking her fingers sharply.

Before she could even move a single muscle, Kadija was suddenly wrapped, from head to toe, in what looked like a mass of spiders' webs, with only her eyes and nostrils still uncovered.

Zach and Shannon stood, open-mouthed as Miss Fletcher slowly walked towards Kadija. "Count yourself extremely fortunate not to have suffered the same fate your friend has. I've enough paperwork to fill in for the school now as it is after that little - *ahem!* – accident with Master Panesar!"

"How is she able to do this?" Shannon murmured as she watched the teacher sweep her hand to the side, causing the mummified figure of Kadija to stick to the wall, before turning to look back at Zach and Shannon.

"I'm not altogether sure..." Zach said, hesitating, before a sudden realisation hit him, "Sorry, Shan... but I think it was you who inadvertently caused it!"

Chapter 20

"Me, how?" Shannon whispered, all too aware of the fact that Miss Fletcher was now stood looking at them, her head tilted slightly as she tapped a long, bony finger against her chin.

"Don't you remember the last thing you said to Miss Hubbard yesterday?" Zach said, adding, "You called Miss Fletcher your *'wicked witch of a teacher'*!"

"Oh really? How delightful! What an irony!" Miss Fletcher laughed, "Undone by your own insolence and stupidity. Don't worry, I've spent years, hoping and praying for this moment. I'll no longer be denied what's rightfully mine. Now I will finally be free of having to spend my time surrounded by lowlife scum like you and your filthy friends!"

Miss Fletcher raised her hands high above her head and took a step forward toward them both.

Shannon sobbed, closed her eyes and held her breath, anticipating the worst as Zach looked down, suddenly aware of the pressure which was being exerted on his hand. He was pleasantly surprised to see Shannon's hand gripping his tightly.

You pick your moments, Zach thought ruefully as he looked back up at the demonic looking face now standing right in front of him.

"Please tell us one thing though, Miss," Zach said, desperately trying to buy them both some precious time, hoping that a solution to their desperate predicament would soon be forthcoming, "Why do you hate us so much?"

"Because," Miss Fletcher scowled, "I was meant for so much more than just teaching a bunch of *oiks* like you. My father promised me greatness, he had it all planned, my life mapped out for me…"

Miss Fletcher hesitated and pointed at Grammarticus. "He even tricked that old buffoon Hubbard into translating *Educalis Totalis* for us! Grammarticus was supposed to set the likes of us apart…get me through my degree…gain me a first! I could have then gone anywhere, done anything, been anyone. Instead, I just about scraped a 2:2! My father still had to pull a few strings just so I could become a *teacher*. That's how I ended up in stuck in this… this…this…godforsaken *dump*!"

Zach could see the anger and frustration glowing in her eyes as she spat each of her words out.

Then it suddenly dawned on him.

Grammarticus was supposed to help *all* the lodge's children get ahead in life, not just those who were still in their local schools.

It was also supposed to help the lodge's older children, those who were at college and university, like Mr Hubbard's friend's only daughter…Miss Fletcher!

Zach could feel a faint flicker of an idea dimly spark in his head, a possible way out of this whole messy situation. "But I still don't understand how not being able to use Grammarticus affected you so."

"No, you wouldn't," hissed Miss Fletcher, "Because the very notion of you ever attending any university is totally beyond your pitiful, working-class brain."

Streaks of green mist still lingered around her fingers as she absent-mindedly twirled one of the classroom chairs around and around in mid-air, alongside Grammarticus, whilst she spoke.

"Maybe," Shannon nodded, suddenly beginning to understand what Zach was trying to do, "But if we do go to university, I bet we could get *firsts* even without the book were we ever to be in the same situation as you."

It was a risky tactic, but they knew that their only hope was to try and provoke their teacher, hoping she'd let her guard down momentarily and make a tiny error of judgement or mistake that they could hopefully capitalise on.

Luckily, Miss Fletcher's ego and ire helped create such an opportunity for them.

"Oh, really?" Miss Fletcher screeched, "So you'd have confidently stood and presented a historical talk at one of the country's leading universities, the only woman out of thirty students, for fifteen minutes then without Grammarticus' help?"

"Absolutely," Shannon chided, "And I'm really surprised that you weren't able to do so too, given your obvious elegance, eloquence and self-confidence."

Miss Fletcher's lip trembled, a momentary chink in her steely, cold-hearted armour, obviously recalling long-past events which were still raw, painful and real to her, despite the years since they'd occurred.

"I am now," she whispered, "But I wasn't then. Grammarticus was supposed to give me the ability to speak verbosely and fluently, without deviation or hesitation. But without it, I stumbled, stammered and blustered my way through the entire thing. I can still hear them all laughing at me, those vile and beastly men, who weren't fit to be in the same room, let alone university, as me! All of them all coming from a much lower social-standing than me too!"

Zach and Shannon looked at each other. Now was their chance.

"I bet you felt so embarrassed," Zach said.

Miss Fletcher nodded. "I did."

"Ashamed?" Shannon asked.

"Absolutely," Miss Fletcher agreed, having tossed the chair aside, spinning the web-bound figure of Kadija around and around with her magic instead.

"Humiliated," Zach said, trying desperately to sound sympathetic.

Miss Fletcher sobbed. "Yes, humiliated and mocked unmercifully to boot"

"I bet you just didn't know where to put yourself that day, did you, Miss Fletcher?" Shannon urged, now going in for the kill, sensing that the teacher was weakening and more vulnerable than ever.

"No, I didn't!" Miss Fletcher wailed, throwing her hands into the air, causing Kadija's mummified form to fall to the floor, "They cackled with laughter, like hyenas, whilst I floundered helplessly before them."

"I bet you wished that you could have been somewhere – anywhere - else but standing there in front of them, didn't you, Miss?" Zach urged.

"Yes…yes…" Miss Fletcher, "It was truly horrible. Even now, all these years later, I wish that the ground had just swallowed me up and saved me from…"

The old teacher suddenly stopped and stared into the eyes of the two children who were now grinning back at her.

"Oh, how very clever…*Bum!*" Miss Fletcher screamed as suddenly a giant sinkhole appeared in the classroom floor, sucking her and most of the desks around her down into it before quickly closing again, Zach diving to catch Grammarticus as it too fell. Shannon rushed over to Kadija and tore the webbing off her friend's mouth.

"Quick," Kadija said, relieved to finally be free again, "Let's get out of here before that old dragon figures out how to get free again…"

"Kadija!" Zach screamed.

But it was already too late.

Suddenly there was an almighty rumbling from deep within the bowels of the Earth, like the sound of tectonic plates crashing against one another, as the very floor beneath them cracked and shook apart again.

"Why did you have to go and say that for?" screamed Zach, before turning for the door, "After all we've been through, haven't you learned anything?"

"Sorry!" moaned Kadija as Shannon quickly grabbed her and followed Zach, just as a torrent of molten fire burst through the floor and filled the air around them. The flames were immediately followed by an enormous, scaled beast which slowly emerged, its tongue forked, its eyes slitted, its horned head carrying more than a passing resemblance to the teacher they'd so patiently and cleverly despatched just moments before.

The Fletcher-Dragon roared as it cast its eyes in their direction. Although transformed, there was no doubt it recognised both the terrified children and the tome that Zach clutched tightly to his chest, the skin on his knuckles tight and white from the grip.

"*Nooooooooooooooooo!*" the Fletcher-Dragon hissed as it pulled itself out of the ground, its wings unfurling, knocking out all the classroom's windows as the children ran out into the corridor.

"Where to now?" Shannon screamed as they ran, their pathway mercifully clear, the majority of the school still being at lunch.

Only a few adults and pupils watched in confusion and bewilderment as the three friends sprinted for the stairs.

However, they too fled when the Fletcher-Dragon finally burst out through the classroom door, taking the entire wall with it as it began to angrily prowl after the children as they began to descend the stairs. By now, Zach, Shannon and Kadija were taking two steps at a time, desperately trying to put some distance between them and the smoking beast.

But they could feel the air around then gradually getting warmer from the heat of the Fletcher-Dragon's body, the staircase juddering from the weight of the creature as they hit the final flight of stairs.

"Under here," Zach shouted, grabbing Shannon, climbing into the narrow gap under the stairwell, Kadija following closely behind.

Through the gap in the stairs above their heads they could see the Fletcher-Dragon's shadow on the stair wall, before the steps themselves creaked and groaned as one taloned foot followed another, dust and debris dropping from the stairs onto the upturned faces of the children below it.

Shannon put a finger to her lips, encouraging Kadija to stifle a sob as the Fletcher-Dragon reached the bottom of the stairs, the screams of those fleeing before it growing distant as they fled in terror away from the beast.

A low growl of discontent rumbled in the bowels of the Fletcher-Dragon as it began to slowly meander towards the front of the school, its snout low to the ground, sniffing out the children, seeking them and Grammarticus out.

Zach held his breath as he watched tens of people escape the building, the Fletcher-Dragon oblivious to, and uninterested in, them as doors flung open, pieces of furniture scattered, arms flailed and loud voices screamed as pupils and staff ran from the hulking creature behind them, cramming themselves through the double-glass doors, packed together, like sardines in a tin.

"Wherrrrrrre?" the Fletcher-Dragon snorted, thick, acrid smoke escaping its nostrils as it approached the barrier before it.

The beast raised its head, its horns gouging the ceiling as it inhaled deeply, before exhaling violently, its flames so bright and fierce that the children hiding under the stairs still had to shield their eyes despite their concealed vantage point.

In seconds, the front of the school was no more than charred embers and liquid metal as the Fletcher-Dragon skulked, its tail swinging angrily back and forth, across the scorched and blackened ground outside.

Zach, Shannon and Kadija sat in the darkness as the screams grew more distant, an occasional roar of anger punctuating them until an eerie silence fell on the school and its surroundings.

"Has it gone?" Kadija finally said, a lump of fear still wedged deep in her throat, almost choking her words as she spoke.

"I think so," Zach whispered.

"Then read that damned book again," Shannon urged, "Please hurry, Zach, we don't know what time we have left."

Zach placed Grammarticus down on the floor before retrieving his phone from his pocket. He turned its flashlight on and held it over the book.

"It's no good," Zach moaned, "I need more light. I'm going to have to crawl out from under here. You two stay hidden and keep an eye out for me."

"Oh, don't you worry about that!" Kadija replied, "You'll have to drag me kicking and screaming from under here whilst that thing's about!"

Zach made to move out of their crawlspace when he felt a hand gently touch his forearm.

"Be careful," Shannon whispered, softly kissing his cheek.

"Don't you worry, I will," Zach said, grateful that the darkness was hiding his blushes as he inched further away from the stairs.

He waited until he was about six feet from the stairwell, until the title 'Grammarticus' became totally visible on its cover, before he dared open the book to cast his eyes over its contents again.

But Zach was dismayed to find that what text was left in the book was even more faded than he previously remembered.

"There's still not enough light," Zach moaned as he fumbled for his phone before flicking his flashlight app on again. He held it above Grammarticus as he flipped page after page, growing more desperate with every turn.

"Anything?" Shannon asked, her eyes fixed on the ruins of the school entrance. In the distance, the sound of sirens was quickly extinguished by a thunderous roar before an eerie silence descended once more.

"Not a damned thing," Zach sighed, slamming the book shut, "This is hopeless, I can't do this! She's beaten us and now she's even more of a monster! Fletcher's won!"

"You can, Zach," Shannon said calmly, "Please try, if only for me."

"Oh God! Fetch me the sick bucket!" Kadija sniffed, "I think I'd rather be eaten by that damned thing than have to listen to you two simper over each other so!"

But his friend's stern rebuke seemed to energise Zach as he opened Grammarticus again, drawing his eyes closer to its pages as he squinted as hard as he could, desperately trying to focus on the few lines of text that still faintly remained.

"How can I read between the lines," Zach muttered, "When I can't even see any in the first place! It's like I'm having to look for a needle in a... Wait! I think I see something!"

"What?" Kadija and Shannon asked in unison, desperate to see Zach's revelation for themselves.

"Words," Zach replied, lowering his phone's light closer to the page, "Lots of them. They're just starting to appear before me."

Zach stared in amazement at the double-page, situated midway through Grammarticus as it suddenly began to fill with a multitude of sentences, all seemingly written by a different hand to the original script he'd read weeks before.

Almost as soon as the new script appeared, the text previously written there faded away, forgotten like a bad joke told by a failing comedian in a half-empty theatre.

It read;

For those who wish to lift Grammarticus' curse,

And to send the art of word's magic into full reverse,

Then carefully recite this hidden text aloud, line by line,

Taking care to utter them using the correct rhythm and rhyme,

As you would when reciting poetry or singing the lyrics of a song,

But beware those who carelessly recant these words wrong,

For Grammarticus' text and power are mystical and unique,

Misquoting them will forever change the way people speak,

Quote carefully - for second chances there are none,

For what is then done can never then be undone...

"I can see it!" Zach screamed as he watched the hidden words become bolder under the flashlight.

"Zach..." Shannon whispered, a slight tremble echoing in her voice.

"In a minute, Shan," Zach replied, his eyes scanning the words a second time as he prepared to recite them to hopefully end this accursed day once and for all.

"Zach...please."

"Just another moment, Shan," Zach begged again, before suddenly stopping and turning his head in the direction of a plaintive cry.

Except it wasn't Shannon who'd cried for his help. The plea had come from Antonio, still dressed exactly like his grandmother, but now suspended by his black cardigan from the fangs of the Fletcher-Dragon, who now stood in the destroyed entrance to the school.

"I'm sorry, Zach," Antonio whimpered, "I tried to run, but the elastic gave way in my nonna's knickers and I tripped and fell. I just couldn't get away from it in time."

"It's OK, Antonio," Zach said, standing to face the beast who held his friend tightly between its teeth.

"*Grammarticusssssssss*," the Fletcher-Dragon hissed, sharply tilting its head back, tossing Antonio's frail body about in the air like a rag doll as it did so.

Zach looked at Shannon and Kadija who had now crawled out from the safety of the stairwell and mouthed 'Sorry' to them as he lifted the book from the floor.

The girls smiled wanly at him as he took a tentative step forward toward the hideous beast whose chest rose and fell in triumph.

"Stop!" Antonio suddenly shouted. "Zach, are you absolutely certain that you can reverse all of this and send everything back to how it was before?"

"Yes," Zach replied, seeing his friend's familiar defiance shine in the eyes of the old woman who hung, like a broken puppet, from the jaws of the Fletcher-Dragon that towered above him, "Well, I'm almost certain."

"Then do it! Toast this bit-"

But Antonio's final words were quickly drowned out, first by the roar of anger that the Fletcher-Dragon growled, then by the sound of it swallowing him whole as Zach began to recant the words that Grammarticus had revealed to him.

"For those who wish to lift Grammarticus' curse," Zach tearfully said, all too aware that the beast's legs were quickly eating the ground beneath them as it made its way toward him, *"And to send the art of word's magic into full reverse..."*

"Zach, come back in here!" Shannon screamed, reaching out a hand toward him, "You'll never read it all in time before it reaches you!"

Zach continued to read aloud but glanced up. He was horrified to see that the Fletcher-Dragon was now just a matter of metres away from him.

"Taking care to utter them using the correct rhythm and rhyme," Zach shouted, knee-sliding across the polished wooden floor into the crawlspace, just as the Fletcher-Dragon slammed a foot down on the exact spot that Zach had just occupied.

"Well, ain't this just peachy!" Kadija cried, "We're trapped, exactly where that thing wants us the most. *'Excuse me Kadija, how would you like to be cooked today? I can barbecue you all ways, as long as you like it well done!'*"

"It won't hurt us, Kadija," Shannon said calmly, quickly placing herself between the mouth of their crawlspace and Zach, "It daren't run the risk of destroying Grammarticus."

Shannon was right, at least in part.

As Zach continued to frantically read the newly discovered verses, stumbling over and repeating the occasional word, the Fletcher-Dragon snorted, huffed and prowled a short distance away, now seemingly unsure as to what it should do next.

"*Sssssssssstop!*" it demanded, its movements starting to become more erratic and desperate as Zach neared the end of his incantation. Then it stopped, perfectly still, seeming to sense that all was soon to be lost. Suddenly, the Fletcher-Dragon reared up high on its hind legs, before pitching its front ones down on the stairs above the children, its claws embedding themselves into the steps as it flapped its huge, skeletal wings and flew backwards, taking the entire flight of stairs away with its taloned feet, revealing the three frightened figures huddled closely together beneath them

"Our Father, who art in heaven..." Kadija sobbed as the Fletcher-Dragon tossed the ruins of the stairs to one side and hovered above them, its leathery wings flapping effortlessly.

"*Grammarticusssssssss!*" it screeched as the creature suddenly swooped down toward them.

"*Misquoting them will forever change the way that people speak,*" Zach panted, desperately trying to recite the last of Grammarticus' verse before the impending fate that was soon about to befall them,

"*Quote carefully - for second chances there are none, What is then done can never be undone!*"

Zach slammed Grammarticus shut and defiantly raised the book above his head, a final futile gesture against their impending deaths as he closed his eyes, feeling the heat of the Fletcher-Dragon's breath on his face as...

Chapter 21

.... First, an eerie silence fell over them, before a sudden cacophony of noise assaulted his eardrums, the sound of dozens of footsteps, followed by the happy chatter of children, occasionally punctuated by the stern rebukes of a few adult voices.

Zach slowly opened an eye and was shocked to find that the crawlspace he was in was still intact. But, more importantly, and unexpectedly, Shannon and Kadija were still huddled together, cowering beside him.

Zach let out a huge sigh and shook Shannon's shoulder. "Shan? It's OK, we did it! We won!"

Shannon looked up, first into Zach's tear-streamed face, then at the restored staircase above them.

"Really? Are you sure the Fletcher-Dragon's gone?"

"I can't be absolutely certain," Zach said, crawling across the floor before standing up and looking at the scene in front of him, "But see for yourself. Come, take a look."

Shannon and Kadija tentatively followed their friend out from their hiding space and gasped.

The school entrance was again intact, looking as it always had, untouched and undamaged. The three of them began to walk toward it, mingling and jostling with the teachers and pupils who were apparently getting on with their normal school lives, just like any other day at George Orwell Primary School.

"We did it!" Kadija cheered, hugging Shannon and Zach, "We saved the world, us and that damned book!"

Zach and Shannon looked at each other and smiled,

choosing not to argue with Kadija's own thoughts and opinions as to her part in Miss Fletcher's magical and mysterious downfall. But their smiles quickly faded as they remembered those who were not there with them to share this moment.

"Yes, that we did, Kadija," Shannon sighed sadly, "But it was at such a terrible cost."

Zach, Shannon and Kadija walked somberly toward the entrance, holding each other's hands, their exhausted and dejected bodies at odds with the noise and laughter now echoing around them.

Suddenly, Zach felt a hand grab his shoulder from behind. He turned and looked into Antonio's beaming face!

Not *Nonna*-Antonio.

No, *Antonio*-Antonio, the cheeky little Italian boy he had met and made friends with on his very first day in Foundation, the *Antonio*-Antonio he had been virtually inseparable from ever since.

"Antonio!" Zach shouted, wrapping his friend in a tight embrace so strong that he could have snapped him in half, "Is that really you? We all thought you were dead…gone…lost!"

"Dude, it's ok. It's me, I'm here," Antonio laughed, "Better watch out world, I'm back!"

Shannon bit her lip as she watched the two boys embrace again, quelling the tears she could feel forming in her eyes. A sudden realisation then hit her. "So, if you're here, Ant, then that must surely mean… Zach?"

Smiling, Zach let go of Antonio as he turned and stared at Shannon, hope again beginning to fill his heart. He nodded and looked at Grammarticus before picking it up and bolting for the stairs.

Antonio, Kadija and Shannon hesitated for a moment before following him, taking two steps at a time as they ran. However, when they reached the top of the stairs, they initially couldn't see Zach.

"There!" Shannon shouted, spotting him crouched in one of the school's numbered guided-reading zones which lined the Key Stage 2 corridor that lay ahead of them, "He's over by that bookcase, there in Level 5."

The three of them quickly ran over to find Zach softly caressing the hand of Chelsea-May, who was sat, her arms tightly wrapped around her knees, which were drawn to her chest. She was humming and rocking gently.

"Chelsea-May! Oh my God!" Kadija sobbed as she grabbed her friend's hand, "I'm so happy you're still alive!"

But Chelsea-May didn't reply at first. She blankly continued to stare ahead of her, as though not noticing anyone else was there.

"Chelsea-May," Kadija repeated, crouching so that she was now at eye level with her friend, "It's all right, it's over. We're here, you're safe again now."

Chelsea-May stopped humming and rocking as she suddenly appeared to recognise her friend's voice. She swallowed hard as though too terrified to speak, looking closely at the back of her hands, turning them over before rubbing her face with her palms.

"Did you see what she did? She turned me into a pig, the rotten old cow!" Chelsea-May said, before finally bursting into tears, Kadija quickly wrapping her arms around her, consoling her friend as the tears soon fell in torrents.

Zach, Shannon and Antonio could only stand and watch as the two girls rocked in each other's arms, joy and relief pouring out of them in equal measure. Shannon turned to Zach and held his hand. "Come on," she said softly, "There's one last place we need to look, Zach. We're still missing a friend."

Zach hesitated for a moment, then squeezed her hand, as he looked at Antonio, who smiled and nodded, obviously happy to see his best mate and Shannon together at last.

"Yes, I know," Zach replied, inhaling deeply, "Let's hope Dev's in there and that this nightmare will finally end."

"Stay here, you three," Shannon smiled, "No need for you to come. Just stay here and wait."

Slowly, Zach and Shannon turned and began to walk towards Miss Fletcher's classroom at the very end of the corridor.

"Hang on a minute," Kadija suddenly cried, "What if you're wrong? What if Fletcher's there and, for Dev, it's just too late."

"There's always hope," Zach smiled, the thought having already crossed his mind once or twice before, "Just think - we're here together again, the five of us."

Kadija nodded sadly. "True but it was different for Dev - Fletcher totally *Thanos*ed him - turned him into a pile of dust."

Zach turned to Shannon and gripped her hand a little tighter.

Shannon smiled. "Well, there's only one way we're going to find out. Come on, Zach, let's go see!"

Zach nodded his agreement as the two of them took a

deep breath and walked briskly towards Miss Fletcher's room, their hearts pounding, their pulses racing as their three friends looked on hopefully but anxiously behind them.

When Zach and Shannon reached Fletcher's room, they stopped just outside of it and pressed themselves against the corridor wall.

Inside they could hear laughter.

Two voices.

One old, one young.

One familiar, one not so.

Both male.

"I'm not certain, but I think that's Dev," Zach whispered, "But I'm not sure whose voice the other one can be?"

Shannon shook her head. "One thing's for certain, it's not Miss Fletcher! It's most definitely a man."

Suddenly, the conversation inside stopped.

Zach and Shannon held their breath as they heard footsteps slowly approach the door.

"I'm sure I heard someone…" the younger voice said, before, sure enough, the all-too-familiar head of Dev poked out the doorway, "I knew it! It's my friends, Zach and Shan!"

The three of them hugged one another, relief overwhelming each of them as time seemed to momentarily come to a standstill.

"It's so good to see you, Dev," Zach said, his voice muffled by his friend's shoulder, "I wasn't sure if… Wait! You don't smell!"

Dev slapped his friend on the back and winked at Shannon. "After watching me disintegrate, that's the only difference he's able to tell!"

"No," Zach blustered, "What I meant to say was...oh, never mind. I'm so glad that you're OK too."

He hugged his friend again, more tightly this time, checking to make sure that Dev was real and that there were no after-effects from him being turned into a mound of ashes. Fortunately, there appeared to be none – at least not outwardly at any rate.

Dev broke free from his friend's grasp and stood back, a more serious expression suddenly masking his olive complexion.

"Only because of you guys," Dev said solemnly before his tone lightened again, "There's someone else here who'd also like to thank you two."

Dev turned and walked through the door, gesturing for Zach and Shannon to follow him.

Shannon looked at Zach and shrugged her shoulders as she walked after Dev, Zach following closely behind her.

As the three of them walked into the once familiar surroundings of Miss Fletcher's classroom, Zach noticed that there were now several subtle differences to it.

For starters, the tables had now been put together into five equal groups, whereas previously it had been two pupils per table, formally arranged in rows.

The room also seemed much lighter and more welcoming, the walls strewn with a range of different English displays, all aimed at helping those in class, rather than leaving them staring at blank, desolate areas devoid of all colour and interest. This was a particularly favourite trick of Miss Fletcher's, believing that her pupils should have no distractions of any kind, blaming their low aptitudes and poor attention span for this.

However, the biggest difference Zach noted was at the front of the class where Miss Fletcher's obsessively tidy *Furniture World* style desk had been replaced by a dark wooded, antique one, its green-leather surface inlay covered with post-its, scraps of paper and a multitude of exercise and textbooks.

At the desk sat an elderly man, his grey hair and goatee beard neatly clipped close to his head and chin whilst his steel-blue eyes, filled with warmth, kindness and compassion, fondly watched as Zach, Shannon and Dev sat on a table-top in front of him.

"Hello, children," the man said gently, his voice rich, smooth and melodic, "It's good to finally speak with you. I apologise for my dishevelled appearance during your last visit."

"Mr Hubbard?" Shannon asked, suddenly recognising the man that sat in front of them, "That is definitely you, Mr Hubbard, isn't it?"

The old headteacher pushed his high-backed leather chair away from the desk and began to walk around it. Zach and Shannon could only look on in disbelief as he slowly sat on the edge of his desk and warmly smiled back at them.

"Yes, it is young lady," Mr Hubbard said, as he pointed at the book Zach still held tightly in his hand, "Because of your bravery, many like me, silenced by Grammarticus, have been freed, again finding their true voice."

Zach looked down at Grammarticus, which now seemed less impressive than ever before. He flicked open the book to the pages where he'd found and read the hidden verse in what seemed to be a lifetime ago, but, in reality, was just a few minutes previously. Zach smiled and shook his head as his eyes fell on the now blank paper he found there.

"With everything that's happened over the last few weeks, Sir," Zach said wearily, "We really had little or no choice."

Mr Hubbard frowned and nodded, placing a reassuring hand on Zach's knee. "There's always a choice. You could have used the book for your own ends once you knew its secrets and history."

"True," Shannon said, looking at Zach and Dev before grinning broadly, "But being as articulate and intelligent as we became was not all it was cracked up to be!"

"Well, I thank you," Mr Hubbard smiled, extending a hand toward them, "Without realising it, you've hit the reset button. Many of us are eternally grateful."

Zach, Shannon and Dev awkwardly shook the old man's hand as he passed them.

Mr Hubbard then lifted Grammarticus from Zach's hands and flicked through its now barren pages, smiling knowingly to himself as he took the book and walked over to the cupboard.

The children watched as Mr Hubbard produced a shredder from it, plugged the machine into the wall and began to tear the pages out of Grammarticus, one by one.

There was the satisfying whirr of the shredder's blades as it slowly began to eat the contents of the magical book which had caused them all such mischief and mayhem.

Suddenly, a cold chill ran down the length of Zach's spine. "Stop, Mr Hubbard! If Miss Fletcher discovers what you're doing, she's bound to become even more twisted and hateful!"

Mr Hubbard paused for a moment before setting the book down beside him. "It's all right Zack, it's over, you also ended Miss Fletcher when you ended the curse."

Zach felt confused.

How could he have done?

Dev, Antonio and Chelsea-May had all returned to normal after the spell had been broken.

And Mr Hubbard appeared to be as he once was.

Would it not be the same with Miss Fletcher?

As though reading Zach's mind and thoughts, Mr Hubbard continued to explain. "Miss Fletcher was pure evil. And, as with all the other mischief unleashed, she was undone when you read that verse."

Mr Hubbard tore another couple of pages out of the book and fed them into the shredder, appearing to be satisfied with himself that the subject was now finally closed.

But Zach wasn't convinced, suddenly realising that there was still something else that was now different about the world around them.

Something different about him.

Something different about his friends.

Something Grammarticus had changed in them all.

"You're saying," Zach began, "The book chooses who it wants to help and who they are to be? Like us still speaking without using any slang or eye-dialect?"

Mr Hubbard tossed his head back, laughed and clapped his hands excitedly. "Exactly, Zach! Look at how your vocabulary has increased and how you have expanded your intellect!"

Zach went to challenge Mr Hubbard again, but stopped, not altogether sure as to whether he was completely satisfied with the answers he had been given by the old headteacher.

It still felt to him that although life would now be infinitely better than it had been before, this still wasn't the world that he once knew. As he struggled to come to the terms with that prospect, Shannon gently grabbed his elbow.

"Come on Zach, let's skip school and go home. I think we've all had enough, at least for today."

"Normally, I'm against such a thing, but go," Mr Hubbard shouted above the sound of the shredder as he fed the hungry machine yet more of the pages from Grammarticus, "However, there's one last thing I have to say…"

Zach, Shannon and Dev looked at one another as Mr Hubbard stood up, clicking his back as he did so.

"Apart from the way you speak, is there anything else about you all that's different and of note?"

The children searched each other's faces, looking for some clue as to what the old headteacher may be alluding to.

"Such as," Mr Hubbard continued, realising that Zach and the others weren't going to be able to give him an answer anytime soon, "a permanent side effect caused by reading the hidden verse that was once wrote?"

Zach, Shannon and Dev again looked blankly at one another as Mr Hubbard smiled and shook his head.

Suddenly, Shannon gasped, "Oh my God, I've just realised! Since the curse ended, we've been doing it all the time…"

Zach swallowed hard at this final twist; at this one, last hidden truth which suddenly hit him like an express train. He slumped to his knees and hung his head in his hands.

"I didn't recite Grammarticus' final verse correctly, did I? Now we're forever cursed to speak to each other only in rhyme…"

Also by Jonas Lane

Slipp In Time
Slipp, Sliding Away
Nona's Ark
Dragonchasers
Another Time, Slipp!

Also by Jonas Lane's Young Writers

Write Here...Write Now!
Bonechillers
Magic, Mischief and Mayhem
Scary Stories

All book titles available to purchase from
www.JonasLaneAuthor.com
or by ordering from amazon.co.uk

Slipp In Time

Living in the sleepy village of Codswallop, adventure-hungry Alex McClellan and his cousin want nothing more than for something, anything, exciting to happen to them. More often than not, however, they end up disappointed.

Then one quiet Saturday, whilst delivering newspapers, they meet the eccentric Lord Thyme-Slipp, who tells them tall-tales about his inventions, including his very own time machine. Despite being given a brief time-trip, they remain unconvinced and return home to find things to do to stop them being more bored than usual.

As they are playing on the computer, fate intervenes. They realise that their only hope in undoing the damage that they have done is to put their trust and belief in the kindly old man and travel back just a few hours in time. But a raging storm and a nervous cat propel them hundreds of years into the past, back to a far simpler time and place in history, causing yet more chaos on their arrival.

There they face a race against time to sort out the mess that they have created, before trying to find their way back home again...

Slipp Sliding Away!

Slipp, Alex and Georgie are back! Literally!
Our misadventurers are back in the present day. But home is a whole different world now from the one that they left less than twenty-four hours before.
Returning to school after the summer holidays, Alex and Georgie are shocked to find that all that they once believed is no more, replaced by an alternative history dominated by a name from the past, of a man that they had briefly encountered before.

Discovering that they may be directly responsible for this strange, new world, the children have no choice but to ask again for help from their kind, but eccentric, inventor friend to right the wrongs caused by their actions. Using his not-so-technical no-how, Slipp has now modified the Time Skipper to help take them back to the exact time and place in the past where fate intervened to change the future.
But a careless mistake and a simple coincidence disrupts their plans as they find themselves pitched into the middle of a deadly argument between two powerful and ambitious men who hold the fate of a kingdom in their hands…

Slipp Sliding Away is the highly anticipated sequel to the acclaimed debut novel, *Slipp In Time.* Building on a world where fun, action and adventure sit alongside nonsense, history and time-travel, Jonas Lane has plunged his characters back into a long-lost time once again that will engage and educate readers of all ages, old and new.

Nona's Ark

Twelve-year-old Nona Lancaster thought that her life was finally on the up, having moved to the school of her dreams where she got to spend her entire day playing sports with her best friends.

However, a sudden, final unexpected and unwanted gift from her secret grandfather soon turned her life on its head.

Faced with a desperate race against time to thwart her new brother's evil plans for the zoo that she too now owned, Nona and her friends embark on the adventure of a lifetime to rescue the animals her grandfather had devoted his life to...

A madcap story in the style of the 1950s Ealing Comedies featuring school children, wild animals and an eccentric head teacher, *Nona's Ark* is an adventure for all ages!

Dragonchasers:
Book 1 - The Knight School

A group of gifted youngsters presented with the chance of a lifetime when offered the opportunity of a free scholarship at one of England's finest, but most elusive, schools.

An ancient evil hiding amongst us, having watched, and plotted our demise for thousands of years, waiting for the moment to strike again.

A secret society tasked with defending humankind, protecting us from a legendary enemy who seeks to return from the shadows and reclaim a world they believe to be rightfully theirs once more.

Part Harry Potter.
Part Da Vinci Code.
All action and adventure, *The Knight School* is the first, gripping adventure in the Dragonchasers series.

Here be dragons...

Another Time, Slipp!

Slipp is back, way, way back!

Having escaped just in the nick of time before the bloody battle of Hastings, Slipp, Alex and Georgie find that they are, yet again, far from home and lost somewhere in time.

Stranded in an England greatly suspicious of strangers, recovering from an attack by one of the nation's deadliest rivals, our misadventurers find themselves pitched into a war of words between two of history's most famous and finest heroes and adventurers.

Faced with finding a way to escape the past, as well as fixing a misguided attempt to correct the future, our terrible trio yet again bumble their way through a past-world where words speak louder than actions...

The third Lord Thyme-Slipp adventure, *Another Time, Slipp* picks up exactly where it last left off, catapulting the reader into a pivotal period in English history in this thrill-a-page adventure which excites, entertains and informs in equal measures.

Praise from the readers of Jonas Lane's books

"As an avid reader, I know when I've found something special when I can't pull myself away from a book. I read Slipp In Time in only a few hours and loved every minute of it! I laughed, giggled, had to pause due to said giggling, and then I laughed some more. It's a brilliant story, and I highly recommend it for children and adults alike."

"Loved it! Great to read a kids' book that has pace adventure and humour. Having the main protagonists as a boy and a girl means that any child can identify with the story. What's not to like about time travel on a sofa! Watch out for 'Hamster Ragu' and 'pomegranate shootout'! As an English teacher, this is one I will definitely be reading with my students. Looking forward to the next one.... did I mention the tantalising cliffhanger at the end?"

"A really good adventure of two young children on a journey, including history and good humour. Kids will definitely enjoy this book and with a cliffhanger like that will be eagerly awaiting the next episode and adventure!"

"I bought this book for my 10-year-old daughter. Despite being an avid reader, she always chooses very similar reading styles (cute puppies, girls having sleepovers, blah blah!) Therefore, I wanted to help widen her reading world. Boy did this book fit the brief! Engaging characters and a writing style that made her want a second book immediately! Can't wait for the sequel!!"

"Excellent read from start to finish. Could not stop turning the pages once I started."

"... brilliant for children and teenagers that love an adventure."

"Fantastic book! Bought this for my 11-year-old son to encourage him to read... he loved it and can't wait for more!"

"I bought this for my 9-year-old daughter who loves anything to do with science and time travel! She absolutely loved it and read it in a couple of days. Well written and easy to comprehend and fitting with today's society. Bring on the next one!"

"Bought this book for myself...loved the imagination of the author...would recommend it to anyone who loves to read and put themselves into the story. Look forward to his and my next journey!"

"Fantastic...loved the story and the references to history. Can't wait for the next book to see what's happened. What a cliffhanger!"

"A fantastic read, suited for all ages, with relatable characters and an interesting plot. The book has a brilliant ending that has left me wanting the second instalment already!"

"Amazing and clever storyline that kept my 8-year-old daughter (and us!) hooked!! What a cliffhanger at the end! Cannot wait to read the next one and really hope there will be more. Excellent!!!"

"A very good read for children and adults. Includes time travel, humour and history. I will recommend this book and I think it'll encourage more children to read!"

"Great follow up, well worth the wait, my son loved it!"

"Bought this book for my seven-year-old son. He really enjoyed it, as did I! Believable characters, funny situations with good links to real events in history. We are both looking forward to the next Slipp story!"

"A lovely story, cleverly written. Once you start to read it you can't put it down. Great characters and plot make it seem perfect for a typical British film."

"Brilliant...This should be rated six stars!"

"Really enjoyed this, suitable for all ages, needs to be a film!"

"...most writers write in a similar way, but Jonas Lane doesn't...that's what makes his books unlike any others."
"My children are reluctant readers and this book has engaged both my children aged 9 and 13 to read, my youngest said this book is fun and exciting. My 13-year-old is dyslexic and has read very few books from cover to cover but he read all this one, so thank you for this book being accessible for all, looking forward to the next one."

"A fantastic read, suited for all ages, with relatable characters and an interesting plot. The book has a brilliant ending that has left me wanting the second instalment already!
"Captivating...Just finished reading this novel with my 6-year-old. We loved it and it had her gripped throughout. Loved how the ending left us wanting more. Fortunately, we have the second novel to hand ready to start straight away!

"A very good read for children and adults. Includes time travel, humour and history. I will recommend this book and I think it'll encourage more children to read."

"My teaching assistant bought the Slipp books and read them to my class during lunch. When we started a new genre – adventure stories – in English, my children were so inspired that they created their own time travel stories! These books really helped my class to develop their own characters and problems that they had to resolve. I would recommend this book to all teachers as I was able to help develop and then read stories that my class were very proud of writing."

"Fantastic story about 2 children on an adventure. Loved the story and the references to history. Can't wait for the next book to see what's happened. What a cliffhanger!"

"Fantastic easy read story for all ages, adventure and history all in one. Ends with a great cliffhanger can't wait for the next adventure."

"After reading the first book in this series, both my eldest daughter and I were desperate to get our hands on this next book! Once again Jonas Lane hasn't disappointed with his well-balanced mix of humour and history. The easy to read style of these brilliant books means that my youngest daughter now is wanting to join in. Hopefully, the next one is in the pipeline, so we can all have one each!!!!"

"Super sequel! Great book - my daughter loved it"

"A heartwarming story full of humour, excitement and morality. Written in a dynamic rhythm that keeps you willfully entranced!"

"Five Stars!"

Thanks to all those that have left such wonderful comments. Authors and writers live or die by the reviews given by their readers. Please take a moment to share your opinions and leave a review by visiting the site that you purchased this book from.

Alternatively, visit Jonas at his website as he would welcome your feedback.

www.jonaslaneauthor.com

Printed in Poland
by Amazon Fulfillment
Poland Sp. z o.o., Wrocław

53642911R00112